A B
PR

BY
DRUSILLA DOUGLAS

MILLS & BOON LIMITED
ETON HOUSE   18–24 PARADISE ROAD
RICHMOND   SURREY   TW9 1SR

*First published in Great Britain 1993
by Mills & Boon Limited*

© Drusilla Douglas 1993

*Australian copyright 1993
Philippine copyright 1993
This edition 1993*

ISBN 0 263 78133 X

*Set in 10 on 11½ Linotron Baskerville
03-9306-56420*

*Typeset in Great Britain by Centracet, Cambridge
Made and printed in Great Britain*

CHAPTER ONE

'THERE you go, then, Mrs Turnbull—that ought to set you up for the weekend,' said Lindy, passing a final soothing hand over the postmistress's knotted shoulders. 'Provided you don't try hanging any more curtains, that is.'

'I'll not be doing that, lassie. I've learned my lesson.' She tried a few experimental movements. 'Yes, that's much easier—and physiotherapy's more effective than getting my sister to rub in that smelly stuff from the chemist's. Cheaper too,' she added with unconscious irony. But then how could she or any of the others know that the doctor's daughter was treating them out of the kindness of her heart, because the nearest hospital was twenty miles away and the round trip just about cancelled out all the benefit of treatment? Not that Lindy's efforts were entirely selfless. After all, she had to keep her hand in. 'That's good,' she agreed, keeping a straight face. 'And don't forget to do those neck and shoulder circling exercises. We can't have you tensing up again now I've relaxed those tight muscles. Can you manage the same time on Monday?'

'Aye, I reckon so. Now tell me, how's your father?'

'Working too hard as usual, but things will be easier once the new partner starts work.'

'I hope your dad's not meaning to give up altogether,' said the patient, looking quite fierce. 'Folk around here swear by Dr Dunbar.'

That was praise indeed, coming from the one who scarcely ever had a good word to say of anybody. 'No, he'll still be working half-time,' Lindy told her. 'So there'll actually be more coverage than at present.'

'Quality, not quantity, is my motto,' insisted the postmistress.

Lindy would have loved to say that she'd always thought it was mind your neighbour's business like your own when, right on cue, Mrs Turnbull asked avidly if Lindy had heard any more details of the butcher's wife's mysterious illness.

Lindy told her she hadn't heard a thing, which was the reply she would have made even if she had — adding with a stifled smile that she felt sure the whole town was wishing the poor lady a speedy recovery. Such tact was no use at all to the town gossip, who was obliged to leave unsatisfied.

Lindy hung up her white coat and tidied the consulting-room ready for evening surgery. Then, having locked up all but the patients' entrance, she went to check on Meg's efforts in the guestroom. A quick look round revealed dust on the bedside table and no towels. That attended to, Lindy went downstairs again to put the supper casserole in the oven.

Meg, their cherished daily at Downside House, had wanted to put flowers on the dressing-table, but Lindy had vetoed that. For one thing, the new partner was a man, and for another, he was only staying with them because there wasn't a decent room to be had in the town at such short notice. The tourist season was well under way and, apart from its own considerable charm, the little Border town of Eyretoun-on-Tweed was right on a popular north/south route.

At the turn of the stairs, Lindy paused and frowned. Her father's bulky black bag was not on the hall table where it should have been at this time of day. He'd done it again—was missing his tea and would go straight into evening surgery without a refreshing cuppa.

Thirty years of selfless service to the community had been rewarded with a serious coronary; hence the need for another partner in addition to his cousin, Dr Ellen Frew. Pa had only been allowed back on condition that he worked no more than half-time in future, so it was fortunate that Dr Balfour had been free to start so soon. Lindy sighed. As well try to semi-retire a racehorse, she surmised.

A shadow loomed on the frosted glass of the vestibule door and she smiled her relief, only to frown again next second when the front doorbell pealed. Not her father after all.

The man on the other side of the door was tall, lean, attractive and dressed impeccably in casual but up-market country clothes. A stranger, and one more than capable of exciting her eager curiosity. 'Good afternoon. How can I help you?' she asked brightly.

Her offer seemed to nonpluss rather than reassure him. He looked round as if to make sure he'd rung the right doorbell before saying, 'I want to see Dr Dunbar.'

'I'm afraid he's still out making house calls,' explained Lindy, 'but if it's an urgent matter I might be able to contact Dr Frew.'

'Thank you, but it's Dr Dunbar I wish to see. I'm——'

'The surgery door is at the back—round to the left.'

'So it says on the sign at the gate,' returned the man, eyeing Lindy with the beginnings of impatience. 'If the doctor is out, then perhaps I could have a word with your mistress.'

'My——?' Lindy gulped, recovered, and gaped at him. He really was rather dishy—and he certainly didn't come across as a double-glazing salesman or a drug company rep. But, whatever and whoever he was, he could hardly be blamed for thinking that somebody wearing an apron and brandishing a feather duster was the hired help. 'There's nobody here but me,' she blurted out, even as she thought what a stupid thing to admit to a casual caller. 'For the moment,' she added firmly. That was when she noticed something not quite right about his hand. The intriguing creature was a patient after all, then. 'Evening surgery starts at half-five, so you've not got long to wait — and the waiting-room is unlocked.'

'But not the surgery itself, I hope,' said the man, his lip curling.

'Unlocked? Certainly not!' Don't say he was an inspector from the Home and Health Department! Hadn't Pa said only yesterday that he'd not be at all surprised if—— 'Oh, look,' Lindy exclaimed with relief as a small white Ford turned in at the gate. 'Here's the doctor now.'

The man had seen it too, and with a few athletic strides he was beside the car as it rolled to a stop behind his own wicked-looking sports job.

A smile broke over Dr Dunbar's gentle, weary face when he got out of his car and recognised the stranger. 'Welcome to Eyretoun, Dr Balfour,' he said, holding out his hand.

Lindy fled to the kitchen as though pursued by fiends. She slammed the door and turned the key in the lock for extra protection. Pa's new partner — and the obvious had not occurred to her; all because he had told her father he couldn't possibly arrive before seven. As much his fault as hers then.

But was it? Was she not the one who had done all the interrupting when he had tried to explain? Understandable, though. Who in the world would expect a partner in a modest country practice to turn up looking like most folks' idea of a millionaire? Should I apologise? wondered Lindy.

She decided to wait and see how he behaved next time they met. In the meantime, a good tea would surely help to smooth him down. Scones still warm from the oven, home-made strawberry jam, shortbread, and one of her special fruit cakes which her chum Bill Galbraith had once said a man might kill for. When the kettle boiled, Lindy filled the teapot and trundled the trolley along the stone-flagged hall to the sitting-room. She opened the door just enough to push the trolley through. 'Lots to do, Pa, so can you look after yourselves?' she called out, being very reluctant to face the new partner again before she'd spruced herself up a bit.

'Come in, please, Lindsay,' her father called back.

When he called her Lindsay, she knew not to argue. She tore off her pinny and threw it on the floor, while running her fingers through her fiery red-gold hair, without improving it one bit. Then she followed the trolley into the room, flushing scarlet up to her large hazel eyes.

'Dear, this is Lyall Balfour, my new partner,' said her father. 'Balfour, my daughter Lindsay, without whom I'd be in a constant state of chaos.'

Dr Balfour was looking as if he found that rather hard to believe, but he shook her hand and in his clipped English tones claimed to be delighted to make her acquaintance.

'How do you do?' she returned with more poise than she felt, adding breathlessly, 'I'm so sorry about the misunderstanding. I should have guessed who you were.'

'Not at all. I should have told you my name at once.'

Except that I didn't give you the chance, Lindy recalled ruefully. 'Never mind,' she said aloud. 'It's all sorted out now, and I dare say you're ready for your tea after driving all the way from London today.'

He acknowledged her eagerness with an indulgent smile that showed his even white teeth. 'Not quite such a marathon — I stayed with friends in Penrith last night. All the same, I shan't be able to resist those delicious-looking scones.'

His tone was as indulgent as his smile, and Lindy squirmed inwardly. He's humouring me, she realised, just as he would a child. That did nothing to repair her wounded self-esteem

Having poured the tea and passed the food round, she sat down quietly on the window-seat and proceeded to look Dr Lyall Balfour over again. Yes, he really was quite something, with his clear-cut, resolute features, deep-set grey eyes, expensively styled short dark hair and obvious self-assurance. If only she hadn't made such a mess of their meeting! Now he'd have her down as gauche and stupid, instead of clever and attractive as she rather desperately wanted him to see her. Now the two doctors were deep in the inevitable shop talk, so Lindy slipped out unnoticed and returned to her kitchen.

Mechanically she prepared the vegetables for supper. She'd formed such a very different picture of her father's new partner. He would be bluff, young and eager — and of course a countryman, who would get quickly on to good terms with all the local folk. Yet Pa and Cousin Ellen had picked this cool, sophisticated Englishman. And if their choice was a surprise, how much more of a surprise was his!

Lindy had been very vexed to miss vetting the short-listed candidates as they came and went for their inter-views that weekend a fortnight back. Unavoidable, though, when one of the physios at the district hospital was getting married that Saturday and all her colleagues wanted to be there. When the superintendent had asked her to act as locum, Lindy had been only too glad to oblige. If she measured up, he'd be more likely to consider her for any vacancy subsequently arising on his staff.

With characteristic impulsiveness, Lindy had thrown up her job in Edinburgh's largest hospital when her father had his heart attack, determined that only she could nurse him back to health. He was much better now, but it wasn't proving as simple as she'd expected to get another post. Not that she was exactly idle. As well as those unofficial physio treatments, she was also filling in for Pa's part-time nurse/receptionist, recently retired and proving very hard to replace.

So much for the vegetables. Lindy was wondering whether a simple fresh fruit salad would be grand enough for one so clearly used to the fleshpots of London, when she was roused by the sound of wheels bumping over the uneven floor of the hall. 'Pa, you shouldn't have,' she was saying when the door opened and she realised it was Dr Balfour who was trying to get the awkward old trolley to go through the gap. She flew to help him. 'This is such a brute of a thing. Every wheel has a mind of its own!'

Between them, they got it parked. 'Thanks, Doctor,' breathed Lindy, 'but really, you shouldn't have bothered.' Why do I feel so — so *rustic* every time I speak to him? she wondered.

He waved aside her protest, assuring her it was nothing. 'I did offer to take evening surgery, but your father insists that I should settle in before starting work. He also said you would show me my room. If you're not too busy. . .'

'No, of course not — this way.' Lindy darted past him into the hall, where she paused wide-eyed, to survey the great mound of top-quality luggage. 'I say, what a lot of stuff you've got! You'll be needing some help.'

'I couldn't dream of allowing you to carry anything so heavy,' he insisted when she went for the nearest thing. 'How about these?' A Burberry raincoat, an overnight bag and a split-new GP's case.

Lindy took them and started up the broad stone stairs. His clothes, his car, his luggage and equipment. . .not at all the trappings expected of a young doctor just starting out in general practice. So what *did* this wealthy sophisticate want with a junior partnership in an obscure country practice so far from his urban southern home? Lindy scented a mystery, but reined in her imagination as she threw open the door of the guestroom. 'From here, you can see almost half our little town, the bridge over the Tweed — that's famous, you know — and right over to the Eildon Hills,' she enthused, harping on the view because it was the best thing about the room. With its heavy Victorian furniture and faded floral carpet, it was almost as it had been in Grandad's day, just like the rest of the house. 'No *en suite*, I'm afraid, but there's a washbasin in the corner and you're right next door to the bathroom. I do hope you're going to be comfortable,' she romped on. 'I'm doing a lamb casserole for supper. Will that be all right?' What the hell's the matter with me? she thought. I'm behaving like an anxious landlady!

When she mentioned the view, Pa's new partner had dumped the cases he was carrying and strolled over to the window. Now he turned round to say, 'The room is delightful, the view is splendid and I'm sure the casserole will be quite as wonderful as your scones.'

Oh, *what* a smoothie! And still talking to me as though I were a child! 'You're too kind,' Lindy returned grandly.

That only served to broaden his smile. 'No, you and

your father are the kind ones, taking me in like this. I only hope I won't need to impose on your kindness for too long.'

She interpreted that as meaning, he wants everything kept on a business footing and is miffed at having to stay here at all. All the same, she could guess what her father would expect her to say. 'We don't mind if you don't, Dr Balfour, so please don't feel you have to take the first hotel room you hear about, just on our account. I'm leaving you to settle in now, but if there's anything at all you need you'll find me in the kitchen.'

No, he definitely wasn't your typical country doctor. Lindy saw him as an up-and-coming consultant type, more at home in some famous London hospital. The sort who was always turning up on the telly when a medical opinion was called for. What on earth would the patients make of him? I've simply got to know why Pa chose him, she decided, and she raised the point the minute her father came in from evening surgery.

'Well now, we short-listed six, as you know,' he began. 'And of those, Balfour seemed to fit in best. Ellen is especially good with children and female problems, I fancy myself as a bit of a physician, and he has concentrated on surgical conditions. Quite a broad range of expertise for a three-handed practice, wouldn't you say?'

'Yes. . .but he's so sophisticated, Pa! How do you think the patients will take to him?'

'That did occur to me, but I got a call to old Mrs Loudon just as he was leaving his interview and he asked if he could come too. I was very impressed by the speed with which he got on to her wavelength. Of course, she remembers his grandfather, so that helped.'

'His *grandfather*? Well, that explains his guid Scots name, but who was this grandfather?'

'He was minister at Eyretoun West Kirk before Mr Aitken.'

'Whoever would have thought it!' breathed Lindy. 'But that's going back a bit. Mr Aitken's been here for just about as long as I can remember.'

Her father smiled and ruffled her hair. 'Which is not all that long. You'd have been about four when old Balfour retired.' His smile faded and he looked rather disappointed. 'You've not taken to Lyall Balfour, have you?'

Now there was a question! 'Oh, I'd not say that, Pa, though he's certainly not what I expected. And I do wish I didn't have the feeling that he's talking down to me all the time,' she added as a tap on the door heralded the man in question. Had he heard? If so, she hoped he wasn't as good at adding two and two as Pa seemed to think he was at his job.

'Please do say if it's inconvenient, Miss Dunbar, but I was wondering if I might have a bath,' said the new man.

'Of course you may, Doctor. There should be lashings of hot water, and you've plenty of time. Dinner'll not be ready for a good half-hour.' Dinner, she'd said, because you could bet your boots there was no such word as supper in his vocabulary!

'He didn't seem to be talking down to you then,' commented Lindy's father when the door closed behind their guest.

'No — because you were here,' retorted his daughter, wishing she'd never tried to put into words the feeling of inferiority he invoked in her. 'Have you taken your pills?' she demanded.

'I'll go and take them now,' said her father, dodging the question, but looking guilty.

'And you call yourself a doctor!' she rebuked him affectionately as he ambled out.

Lindy set the table in the dining-room, using the best silver. They usually ate in the kitchen to save bother—and if Pa lets that out, I'll batter him! she decided as she dashed upstairs to splash cold water on her face and change into a simple shirtwaister of mint-green cotton.

She needn't have worried. When she led the way into the dining-room, her father merely commented on the delicious smells coming from the kitchen.

Dr Balfour was very charming at dinner, taking a second helping of fruit salad and admiring the Ferguson landscape hanging over the massive mahogany sideboard. Lindy continued to be doubtful. He still wasn't treating her as a grown-up, and more than once she'd caught him casting thoughtful glances out of the window at the overgrown garden.

When she carried the coffee into the sitting-room, Dr Balfour sprang up to take the tray from her and put it on the coffee-table before resuming his seat and his shop talk with her father. 'Perhaps you should advertise more widely, John,' he said.

Advertise what? wondered Lindy, as she asked politely, 'Black or white, Doctor?'

'Black, please—and no sugar. Do we know how many fully qualified nurses are living in Eyretoun?'

He had asked her father, but Lindy butted in. 'Seven, apart from the two community nurses.' She plonked his coffee down within reach. 'Not bad for a town of three thousand inhabitants.' She took coffee to her father, then sat down beside him.

Lyall Balfour viewed her with gentle patience. 'But are any of these ladies currently seeking employment?' he asked.

'Three of them are men,' scored Lindy, feeling rather

pleased with herself. 'They're all charge nurses at Haddington Hall—that's the local psychiatric hospital. Then there's Mrs Keir, she's got three wee ones under five, and Mrs Thom's got her mother, and—and. . .' She bit her lip aware that she was only reinforcing his point. That'll teach me to jump into other folks' conversations, she was thinking.

His expression suggested he could be echoing that thought, but he only complimented her on the excellence of the coffee before turning to her father. 'As I was saying, John, it might be worth advertising more extensively—and for a full-time nurse. That might well attract a career girl from outside the town who has no family commitments.'

Oh, very likely, though Lindy, perking up again. She never stayed flattened for long. Did he really suppose that a qualified nurse, footloose and fancy free, would want to bury herself in sleepy wee Eyretoun, with the whole world to choose from? Which thought inevitably set her wondering again why he had chosen Eyretoun for himself.

Her father said, 'You may have something there, lad. I don't suppose you know of anyone who may be interested, do you?'

There was quite a pause before Lyall Balfour said slowly, 'As it happens, I rather think I do.'

Lindy almost choked on her coffee. Pa's new partner might be contriving to look as if he'd only just thought of it, but she'd be willing to bet that was what he'd been leading up to all along. He was planning to import his girlfriend—or his wife!

She was supposed to be meeting a few friends for a drink tonight, but how could she go out and leave Pa unsupported? What other plans was this persuasive newcomer hatching?

'Just look at the time, Lindy!' exclaimed John Dunbar when the clock on the mantelpiece struck half past eight. 'I thought you were meeting the trio tonight.'

'Not necessarily,' she returned. 'Besides, I've still got the kitchen to see to.'

'Nonsense, darling. Away with you now — I'll tidy up.'

'I shall only go if you promise me not to go into the kitchen! You've done quite enough for one day. Promise me, now. . .'

'I promise, if that's the only way to get you to go out and enjoy yourself, but I do wish you'd accept that I'm better now.'

'I will — when you're quite back to where you were before.' Lindy fixed Dr Balfour with a very serious look. 'I'm relying on you to see that my father doesn't overtax himself, Doctor.'

'Isn't that exactly why I'm here?' he asked quietly.

Lindy got home at ten past midnight and went straight to the kitchen, rolling up her sleeves as she went. She stopped in the doorway, open-mouthed. There wasn't a dirty dish in sight, the surfaces had been wiped clean and everything put away.

Next morning she could hardly wait for her father to come to breakfast. 'You promised me you'd not go into the kitchen, Pa — and you did!' she accused in tragic accents.

'Yes,' said the doctor calmly, sitting down and helping himself to cereal.

Lindy wasn't sure, but she thought he was suppressing a smile. 'All right, what have you got to say for yourself?' she demanded.

'I had to, dear. Lyall managed fine until it came to putting things away. Then I had to show him where everything went.'

'You—mean. . .' Lindy sank slowly into her chair, speechless at the thought of elegant Dr Balfour clearing up her cookery chaos in his crumple-free Daks and faultless Italian shirt. She wouldn't have believed he even knew how to work the dishwasher—never mind about getting all the brown bits off the top of the cooker the way he had. 'Well, I'll be——' she began as the man himself came in, loooking as good as a Jaeger ad in faultless cords and a checked shirt, open at the neck. What a lovely Adam's apple he's got, she thought foolishly. Manly, but not knobbly, like Bill's——

'I'm sorry if I kept you waiting,' he said, sliding into his seat.

Lindy pulled herself together and lifted her eyes the necessary inches to meet his quizzical look. 'No, not at all. Pa's only just come down.' She leaned forward earnestly. 'Dr Balfour, it was extremely kind of you to deal with that frightful mess in the kitchen last night. I'm very grateful—and even more ashamed.'

'I've seen worse,' he returned calmly. 'Besides, you did tell me to see that your father didn't overdo things.'

'I meant in the practice! Oh, dear, this is awful!' Now she was flushing and floundering just like the adolescent he obviously thought her—and she was quite unable to stop it. If she only had some idea why he was having this embarrasing effect on her, she might be able to control herself. . .

'I expect Lyall would like something to drink, dear,' her father suggested gently.

'Drink? Oh, yes. . . Tea or coffee, Doctor? I've made both.'

'Coffee, please—if there's enough.' He might or might not be used to the best of everything, as she'd decided, but he was obviously determined not to give any trouble now. Yet last night she'd wondered if he was all set to take over. Lindy scanned his handsome, clear-cut features for clues, realised she was in fact staring and, turning to her father, hurriedly asked him his plans for the day.

He answered her indirectly by saying to his new partner, 'As this is Ellen's weekend on, I thought I'd show you round the district and explain the set-up in more detail.'

'That would be splendid if you have the time, John.'

'Will you be wanting lunch, Pa?' Lindy asked practically.

'That rather depends, dear. We'll see how it goes.'

A typically unhelpful male answer, thought Lindy fondly, but only because it was her beloved father who had made it. 'If you do come back, there'll be soup and salad on the go. Have you warned Dr Balfour what you're planning for this evening?' she asked next, wondering why she couldn't call him Lyall as her father did.

'Not yet.' He turned to Lyall again. 'I've invited a few of the local worthies to come and meet you over drinks and a spot of supper, lad.'

Lyall managed to look pleased. 'That's very thoughtful of you.'

Lindy wondered what this sophisticated townie would make of Eyretoun's foremost inhabitants — and they of him. It would be interesting to watch from her post on the sidelines, dispensing food and drink.

But breakfast was taking too long this morning and Cousin Ellen Frew would soon be arriving for morning surgery. 'Take your time, lads,' she urged, 'but duty calls, so I'm away now.'

Lyall Balfour stopped buttering his toast to look at Lindy with surprise. 'So what else do you do besides running the house so beautifully?'

'Lindy is doing surgery duty for us until we get our new nurse/receptionist,' said her father with pride.

'A young lady of many talents, then,' returned his partner, using that condescending adult-to-adolescent tone again. Just how old did he think she was?

'And I've got three good A-levels too,' she told him satirically.

'Then, career-wise, the sky's the limit,' observed Lyall Balfour kindly.

'Except that I've got no head for heights,' retorted Lindy, getting up from the table and collecting her dirty dishes. Their appreciative laughter followed her out.

There were already three patients in the waiting-room when Lindy went through to the surgery, via the connecting door at the back of the hall. She gave them all a cheery word of greeting. The bank accountant would be wanting another prescription for his indigestion. It was a safe bet that the joiner's boy had misfired with the hammer again—it was a miracle he had any fingers left—and with Mrs McClure, it would be either her back or else her varicosed leg had broken down again. There was a lot to be said for a practice nurse who had grown up in the place. Lyall Balfour's girlfriend, or whatever, would have a lot to learn—and guess who'll be doing the teaching, Lindy was reflecting as Ellen breezed in

'Right, Lindy! Wheel in my first victim,' she called cheerfully as she swept past and into her consulting-room.

Saturday mornings were usually a doddle compared with the rest of the week, and this morning was no exception. Lindy was back in the house by eleven, to find the dining table cleared and the dishwasher fed. Pa and/or Lyall Balfour again? Suave and domesticated. What an intriguing combination!

* * *

The rest of the day was given over to preparing for the evening. Most of the folk who were coming were owed hospitality for all their kindness and help during her father's illness, so Lindy had decided on a buffet supper as well as drinks. So, for days past, nearly all her spare time had been taken up with cooking and freezing. It had been an awful chore but well worth it, she decided, viewing the laden dining table, extended to its fullest, when all was done. The doctors had been back for an hour or more, so with luck the bathroom would now be free. She might even manage a quick dip if they hadn't taken all the hot water.

After her bath, Lindy put on her most sophisticated dress — a draped and flowing creation in muted corals and greens that showed rather a lot of shoulder and bosom. Get an eyeful of this, Dr Balfour, and *then* ask yourself how old I am! she thought. Now for some mascara and plenty of lipstick. . . There! I could easily pass for nineteen and no bother. But when you were twenty-three, was that really such a bonus? Never mind — I'll be really chuffed if I'm still looking younger than I am when I get to forty, thought Lindy, cheering up.

Major and Mrs Wood were the first to come, as Lindy had known they would be. The Major said it was his Army training, while his wife maintained it was all down to nosiness and the fear of missing something. Lindy showed them into the sitting-room and left her father to make the introductions. Loud guffaws minutes later suggested that the evening was off to a good start.

You could always rely on the Eyretoun folk to be punctual, and soon the big sitting-room was stuffed to bursting. Ellen was there by then, so Lindy saw no need to help with the entertaining. Besides, she had more than enough still to do in the kitchen.

She was interrupted in her final preparations by the doorbell. Every invited person was here, so it must be somebody wanting a doctor, decided Lindy, before she opened the front door to find her friend Elspeth Hamilton on the doorstep. 'I was at a loose end, Lindy, so I thought I'd drop by and see if you'd like to go for a bar supper somewhere — only it looks as if you're having a party.'

No marks for smart deduction, Elspeth, with a drive full of cars and others strung out halfway round the town green! 'Shall I just take myself off, then?' Elspeth asked pathetically.

'Come in, you clown,' said Lindy, torn between amusement and exasperation. Elspeth knew all about the party; her outfit was proof. You didn't go out for a bar supper in Eyretoun wearing your only Jean Muir original.

Lindy had told her father that she didn't intend asking any of her friends tonight. That was because the blonde and gorgeous Elspeth — a successful knitwear designer with her own factory — would monopolise the new partner, whatever he was like, thus scuppering the whole point of the party. And if Elspeth wasn't invited, Lindy could hardly ask the other members of the trio; Andy Robertson, the son of a wealthy local farmer, and Bill Galbraith, who was assistant to the local vet. It was Bill's boss who was largely responsible for all the laughter ringing round the sitting-room.

But Elspeth always knew what she wanted and scrupled not to get it, so she'd sidestepped Lindy's thinking and invited herself. 'Now that you're here, you can jolly well come and help me in the kitchen,' said Lindy, forestalling Elspeth's march towards the noise. 'Supper's almost ready, but I still need some help.'

'Of course I'll help you, darling. Why else am I here?'

tinkled Elspeth, conveniently forgetting the bit about the bar supper.

When the guests streamed eagerly into the dining-room in answer to Lindy's summons, there was Elspeth appealingly arranged beside the buffet and managing to look as if it was all her own work. Sometimes I could cheerfully strangle her, thought Lindy, watching Lyall Balfour's appreciative response to the spectacle. And it wasn't the table he was looking at. He had been squiring the minister's wife, but Elspeth soon contrived to take Mr Aitken's place.

Lindy knew she could learn a lot about social success by watching Elspeth at work, but somebody had to make sure that everybody got fed, and as Ellen was now locked in friendly verbal battle with the local chemist Lindy knew fine who it had to be. 'So what can I get for you, Major?' she asked cheerfully. 'Chicken velouté or salmon? I know how much you like salmon — yes, that is dill sauce. . .'

'You're not getting anything to eat yourself,' said Lyall Balfour, materialising at Lindy's elbow some ten minutes later. How on earth had he got away from Elspeth so soon? And, more interesting, why had he wanted to?

'To tell the truth, I was tired of food by the time it was ready,' she admitted.

'That's exactly what my sister always says,' he sympathised. 'But you should have something, so I put this together.' She'd been wondering who the second loaded plate he was carrying was for. 'I hope you like quiche; practically everything else was gone by the time I got to the table. Whatever else they may suffer from, it's plain to me that the good people at Eyretoun have excellent digestion.'

'This is really kind of you,' she said, smiling her

appreciation of his thoughtfulness. She wasn't absolutely averse to the way he was looking at her either.

'You're looking very grown-up tonight, young Lindsay,' he told her, thereby throwing the switch and reversing the approval process.

'Oh, good,' she returned with dangerous calm.

'Your dress is delightful. A little old for you, perhaps — but very becoming.'

'I'm very glad you think so, but all the same, perhaps it would be better to put it away until I'm absolutely grown-up,' she retorted, banging her plate down on the sideboard. 'And now I must ask you to excuse me. I've just spotted old Mrs Telford all alone — and with no food either.'

By the time she had fed the old lady and found her somebody to talk to, Elspeth had homed in on Lyall again, her amazing eyelashes all aflutter. Lindy frowned, retrieved her supper unnoticed and took it with her to eat in the kitchen, while she put the finishing touches to a large pavlova.

'I think that went off very well,' said Dr Dunbar, yawning widely as he shut the front door after the last departing guests. 'And entirely due to your wonderful catering, darling. You really are a magician in the kitchen.'

'Any fool can follow a good recipe,' insisted Lindy, embarrased as always by a compliment. 'Don't lock the door, Pa. Lyall Balfour's not back yet.'

'I didn't see him go out,' said her father curiously.

'He's taking Elspeth home. Surprise, surprise, she somehow forgot to bring her car.'

'What was she doing here anyway? I thought you said——'

'So I did, but you know Elspeth.'

'Yes, she's just like her mother. What a time that woman gave me until your dear mother took pity on me and married me! She stopped then.'

'I wonder if that would stop Elspeth?' mused Lindy. She was also wondering how Elspeth would deal with Lyall's girlfriend when she appeared.

'Marriage? Probably not—not these days.' Another yawn, his second in as many minutes, noted his devoted daughter.

'Up to bed with you, now,' she ordered. 'There'll be all day tomorrow to tidy up. I'm only going to cover what's left of the food and then I'll be turning in myself.'

'Mind you do, Lindy.' It was a measure of his fatigue that he didn't argue.

Lindy watched him go with anxious eyes. She'd never quite recovered from the shock of her mother's premature death six years back, and if she were to lose him as well. . . She shivered, told herself not to be morbid, and after exchanging the dress that was 'too old for her' for jeans and a faded T-shirt, she started to clear the dining-room.

The dishwasher was busy with the first load and Lindy was boxing leftovers for transfer to the fridge when Lyall came into the kitchen. She took a quick look at the clock, to see that he'd been gone less than twenty minutes. She hadn't expected him to come creeping in for hours. Elspeth must be slipping.

She stared when he took off his jacket and put on her plastic pinny. 'No, Doctor,' she said firmly.

For answer, he ran hot water into the sink and reached for the detergent. 'Presumably you're not intending to put silver in the dishwasher.'

'No, but there's no reason on earth why you should do it. Good grief, you've done hardly anything but wash dishes since you arrived!'

'Was or was not the party given for my benefit?' he queried.

'Well, yes, it was — but I'm dressed for this and you're not.' If that suit had cost a penny less than four hundred pounds, then this wee lassie didn't know the value of anything.

He smiled at her over his shoulder. It was a very nice smile, and Lindy was all set to smile back when he spoiled it. 'Yes, that's much more suitable than the dress,' he agreed.

He could have meant either for washing-up, or for her at all. Being Lindy, she went for the second option. 'I'm sure you're right, so you'll be glad to know I've put it away until I'm twenty-one,' she retorted absurdly.

'And how long will that be?' he asked, amused.

Not again in this life, so — 'Too far off to contemplate,' she said, almost relishing the thought of his dismay when he found out — as soon he must — that she was a fully qualified physiotherapist.

'Shall I throw this water out now, or is there anything else you don't want to trust to the mechanical scullery-maid?' asked Pa's new partner.

Lindy had to giggle in spite of being cross with him. 'You could do those crystal dishes — if you insist.'

'Oh, I do,' he said firmly. 'Never leave for tomorrow what you can do today, and all that.'

He might believe that or he might not. At any rate, he seemed to be putting off a very willing Elspeth until another day!

CHAPTER TWO

MONDAY morning surgeries were always extra busy, swollen by the excesses or misfortunes of the weekend. So Lindy ate a hasty breakfast in the kitchen, left everything ready for her father and their guest and scampered through in good time to man the surgery phone. The appointments book was soon full, but how could you turn away such pressing problems as an acute abdominal tenderness in the right iliac fossa, or a child with a temperature hovering around forty centigrade? And if that bruised and swollen foot didn't need X-raying to exclude or confirm a fracture or two, then Lindy wasn't fit to call herself a physio.

The phone rang for the umpteenth time since eight. She listened for a few seconds before saying calmly, 'The doctor will be there as soon as possible — yes, definitely this morning. Yes — Dr Dunbar himself. 'Bye now, Mrs Morrison, and try not to worry.' She dashed off to look out the patient's records before she was interrupted again. She managed that. Would she also have time to ring the community nurse about Mrs Thomson's dressing before —— No. The doctors were coming in now.

Lindy didn't waste time on politenesses. 'Here's your list of visits, Pa. And better make Josh Morrison your first. He's been vomiting all weekend, and from the description there's been some bleeding. Carrie Firth's had another of her attacks, but if she's as breathless as she claims it's not showing in her speech. Betty McKay's varicose ulcer has broken down again, but Phil can drive

27

her in, so I'll give it the once-over and report. And don't forget your pills!

'Now then, Dr Balfour, which would you like first? A possible acute appendix or a drowsy child with a raging temp? They're both ready to be seen.'

A white-coated Lindy in the surgery was not at all the same as Dr Dunbar's domesticated teenage daughter, and Dr Balfour was eyeing her with nothing short of amazement. He needed a deep breath before saying, 'I though that children were Dr Frew's province.'

'Cousin Ellen's out visiting a suspected coronary and will not be back for a good half-hour,' Lindy explained.

'The child, then — please.'

'Yes, Doctor. This room.'

'Thank you — Nurse,' he answered with the hint of a smile.

Priorities settled, Lindy turned away to explain yet again to an irate Mr McCallum that she did indeed know his appointment was for nine, but emergencies always came first. 'Remember that time you fell off your tractor?' she asked as a clincher.

'Miss Dunbar! An ambulance for this child, please.'

'Yes, Doctor, right away. Sorry, Mrs Paterson, I'll look for your scarf in a minute.' Dial. 'Ambulance Control? Eyretoun surgery here. We have a child with query query meningitis for the District General — urgently. Thanks, Tom. Knew we could count on you.' Put the phone back. 'My word, Geordie, that's the best black eye you've collected yet! Bring him into the dressing-room, please, Granny, and let's see what I can —— Next patient? Yes, Doctor. Your turn at last, Mr McCallum. What about that abdominal pain, Doctor?'

'Your diagnosis was wrong, I'm glad to say,' Lyall told her.

'I am glad.' But how superior he had sounded! Still,

he couldn't fault her for suspecting. Back to present matters. 'Now then, Mrs Burns, are you quite sure Geordie wasn't knocked out or even a bit drowsy afterwards?' By now, Lindy had gone into overdrive, and there she stayed for the next two and a half hours. When the last patient left, she made coffee for the doctors.

Cousin Ellen got hers first. 'So how was the rest of your weekend, Ell?' asked Lindy. Her father's cousin might be nearing sixty, but she still liked to be treated as one of the girls.

'Mustn't grumble. Only two calls in the early hours and both of 'em justified. How about yourself?'

'Peaceful. Dr Balfour went out right after breakfast yesterday morning and didn't get back until I'd gone to bed.' And would I not just love to know where he went! thought Lindy.

'That must have been a relief. John says you're not sure what to make of him.'

'Apart from treating me like sweet sixteen, he's all right, I suppose. No, that's not fair,' Lindy corrected. 'He's very nice — and helpful. You should have seen him up to his elbows in sudsy water after the party! It's his reason for coming here that puzzles me.'

'He wants to get back to his roots, dear. It's a Border family, and his grandfather was minister at Eyretoun West for over forty years.'

'Yes, I know all that, but he's so — so *English*, Ell! And if you want my honest opinion, I think he could be hiding something.'

Ellen burst out laughing at that. 'That fertile imagination of yours will land you in trouble one of these days! How can he possibly have anything to hide that's relevant? If he'd done anything professionally naughty he'd have been struck off.'

She should have remembered that Ellen preferred

facts to fancies. Lindy produced one. 'You can't deny the neat way he's persuaded Pa to consider his girlfriend for the post of practice nurse.'

'His sister, dear — his sister. Apparently the poor girl's just been through a divorce, and Lyall thinks the change will do her good. And as she's currently working as a casualty sister at St Crispin's in London, she's not likely to find our little surgery too demanding.'

Thwarted again, Lindy returned to her first subject. 'So you don't see anything odd in somebody who's lived all his life in London suddenly deciding to bury himself in the country?'

'Absolutely not. To me, the only wonder is why he never did it before. London. Bah! Muckle great smelly place.' Ellen piled sugar in her cup and stirred vigorously.

Lindy took the hint. 'I guess I'd better take him some coffee now — and no, I'll not be putting any truth drug in it.' Ellen's raucous cackle followed Lindy out of the room.

Lyall Balfour was seated behind the desk, dictating into a very fancy-looking contraption the like of which Lindy had never seen before. Mrs Gavin, their nice elderly secretary, was in for a shock, accustomed as she was to deciphering the doctors' awful scrawl for transfer to an aged portable Corona. Thinking she'd better not disturb him, Lindy put the tray on his desk and slid it carefully into his line of vision. Then she turned to go.

'Thanks, Lindsay,' he said.

'All part of the service, Doctor.'

'Which is really very good — for the most part.' He switched off and stretched his arms sideways, then relaxed. 'Is it always this chaotic?' he asked mildly.

And she thought the morning had gone so well! 'Monday mornings are always especially busy. In any general practice,' she added. Hadn't he noticed that during his trainee year? Presumably he had done one. Then again maybe not. . .

'Busy, yes — but chaotic?' He reeled off a list of minor hiccups, ending with, 'And I still haven't seen the consultant's report on Andrew McCallum. Would you ask the receptionist to bring it to me now, please?'

Lindy fished the missing letter out of her pocket and put it on the desk, before commencing, 'My apologies, Doctor, but I am the sum total of the morning support staff. I take and make all phone calls, give appointments, find records, do any dressings and act as chaperon — when I can. I'm sorry to hear that the end result of all my efforts is chaos.'

As the recital lengthened, Dr Balfour's well-defined eyebrows were performing acrobatics. 'Good grief, girl, how do you remain sane?' he asked when she reached the end. 'No wonder the phone rang for so long about half an hour back!'

'That would be when I left my post for two minutes to pay the window-cleaner — in my other capacity as housekeeper. Did my father not explain how we arranged things before you came?'

'From the medical standpoint, yes — and that I found very satisfactory, otherwise I'd not have considered coming.'

Was he implying that it was Pa and Ellen who'd been on trial and not the other way about? 'Presumably the satisfaction was mutual,' she murmured.

It was as though she hadn't uttered. 'And naturally I assumed that the administration would be equally satisfactory.'

'But you don't think it is.' Lindy sighed as her natural honesty overcame her resentment. 'I don't know where you've been working, but I guess it was a whole lot smarter and up to date than we are. And I'm very sorry that you think I'm such a muddler.' She ignored his gasp of protest and ploughed on, 'All I can say in my own defence is that this isn't really my line.' This was as good a moment as any for confessing. 'Actually, I'm —'

' — only helping out. I know — your father explained. And I'm not criticising, my dear child, only trying to establish the position.'

How did you tell a man you were a fully qualified professional woman the second after he had called you his dear child? He'd feel such a fool. 'I'm sure you'll be able to devise a better system, along with my father and Ellen. And now, if you'll excuse me, I think I heard the bell. Will you be in for lunch?'

'No, thank you. I'll get a sandwich over the road at the Eyretoun Arms. Incidentally, the receptionist phoned me earlier to say that they've had a cancellation, so I'll be moving in this evening — and leaving you in peace.'

'You'll certainly be very comfortable there, Doctor,' said Lindy as she shut the door. But if you can afford their prices, I'm surprised you need to work at all, she was thinking as she went to deal with Betty McKay's varicose ulcer.

Dr Dunbar eyed his lunch without too much enthusiasm. 'No wonder Ellen prefers to go home,' he remarked obliquely.

'Ellen goes home to feed her cats — and I do know what you think of cottage cheese, Pa, but the fact remains it's good for you. Anyway, I've pepped it up with some fruit. How was your morning?'

He brightened up at that. 'You were quite right about Josh Morrison, dear. He does have a gastric ulcer and should be safely tucked up in hospital by now. D'you know, this is the very first time I've ever finished all my visits by lunchtime? Unless of course more came in later. . .'

'One or two, but His Nibs is doing those. Speaking of whom, he doesn't think much of our admin,' said Lindy.

'That's understandable. We don't think much of it ourselves, do we?'

Lindy shrugged. 'Just letting you know he'll be wanting to discuss it, Pa. And another thing. He's moving to the Eyretoun Arms today — and I'd really like to know how he can afford that. It's sixty pounds just for B and B, you know.'

'I think I can satisfy your curiosity on that point,' said her father, smiling slyly. 'Lyall's father married his boss's daughter — and the boss was head of a family merchant bank. And as Lyall's mother was an only child who died before her father — well, there you have it. Is there any apple pie left?'

Subject closed, Lindy. 'A wee slice, but if you have it now, it'll be yoghurt and prunes tonight.'

'Why is everything that's good for one so damned unpalatable?' wondered Dr Dunbar with a heavy sigh, just as Meg looked in to say that the washer on the cold tap of the bath had gone again. And another thing. That Dr Balfour didn't make a very good job of cleaning it after himself. 'And if there's nothing else, I'm off now, Lindy,' she wound up.

Lindy agreed with all of that, and as soon as lunch was over she called the plumber, cleared the table and then cycled down to the shops to buy a few basics before preparing the consulting-room for her own special patients. There would be five of them this afternoon, and if they went on snowballing like this, she'd need to get her diploma framed and up on the wall next to Pa's!

The first patient, Mrs Gifford, was in a bit of a mood today. 'Ma back's no better,' she stated baldly.

'This is only your third visit, and your back's been bothering you for months, remember.'

'What I think I'm needing is some o' that interference my friend's getting at the hospital for her neuritis.'

'I expect you mean interferential therapy, Mrs Gifford. It's a form of electrical treatment, but it'd not be my first choice for chronic backache.'

'Pain's pain whatever,' muttered the patient.

Lindy wasn't about to risk debating that. 'It takes more than two treatments to make an impression on a back like yours,' she repeated with gentle firmness. 'Let's persist with deep heat treatment and gentle manipulation and if there's no improvement in, say, a couple of weeks, then we'll have to think again.'

'That machine's no' very new,' observed Mrs Gifford, casting a disparaging eye over it.

'But it's a lot more reliable than some of the later models,' Lindy insisted, beginning to wonder if this free treatment centre was quite the wonderful idea she and Pa had thought it. 'Come on now, give it a whirl. The alternative is driving over to Roxburgh three times a week, remember.'

'Aye, there is that,' agreed the patient, beginning to undress at last.

Mr Black came next. He had been discharged from hospital some time back after sustaining a severe stroke. The community service was overstretched, and as he suffered from travel sickness he had declined to go back to the hospital for outpatient therapy. So he had stiffened up. Lindy had despaired when she first saw his tightly clenched fist, but it was wonderful what an ice-bath for the muscle spasm and a prolonged passive stretch could achieve. 'I can hold a fork now that you've padded out the handle for me, miss. D'you think I'll soon be playing the piano?'

Always be careful never to depress the patient. 'Well now, who knows? We'll just have to wait and see, but——'

The old man's eyes were sparkling with mischief. 'That'd be a miracle, lass. I couldnae play it before.'

'Oh, Mr Black, what a tease you are!' laughed Lindy.

'Caught ye there, did I not?'

'You surely did—and now I'm going to catch you in this ice-bath. Just see how your fingers are uncurling. . .'

When Mrs Gifford had had her dose of short-wave diathermy, Mrs Rennie got her arthritic knees done. A lifetime of scrubbing floors for half the town had been largely responsible for their present state. She swore the pain was subsiding, but what she really needed was joint replacements, yet how could she spare the time away from her invalid husband and retarded son? Why did some folk have so much to bear and others so little?

Mr Murdoch was next. 'I can tell you've been doing your loosening exercises regularly at home,' Lindy told him. 'At this rate, we'll have full movement in this shoulder by the time you go back to fracture clinic, and that'll please the surgeon.'

'Not half as much as it'll please me, lass. I'm needing to paint the scullery ceiling.'

Mrs Turnbull was last as usual. 'Is that right that Josh Morrison's away to the hospital to get his stomach out?' she demanded before she was fairly through the door.

'Mr Morrison was certainly admitted this morning, but that's as much as I know,' said Lindy. 'How are you today, Mrs Turnbull?'

'So so. Come on, lassie, you can tell me. You ken fine it'll go no further.'

Ha, ha, ha! 'But I've told you all I know. Perhaps his wife will have some news after she's visited him.'

Mrs Turnbull's lip was curling. 'She's as tight as a bank safe, that one. They're saying he lost twelve pints of blood over the weekend.'

'That can't be right, Mrs Turnbull, or he'd not still be with us. Now then, what about this little problem of yours?'

'Little, is it? You'd not be saying that if it was yours. Oh, what a night I've had!'

Having diverted her so skilfully, Lindy was able to proceed with treatment. Mrs Turnbull was getting ready for another fact-finding session when purposeful steps were heard approaching and the consulting-room door was thrown open. Lyall Balfour checked in the doorway, his expression horrified as his eyes rested on the ancient short-wave diathermy machine. It silenced even the postmistress as she gazed first at his stony face before turning to look at Lindy, who was now rigid with apprehension. She had a fair idea of what was bugging him and was willing him not to say in front of Mrs Turnbull, of all people.

He didn't. 'I wasn't aware that this room was in use,' he said tartly.

'But the other one is free, Doctor.'

'Thank you.' Another black look round the room and a very heavy sigh. 'I'd appreciate a word with you next door, if you please,' he said with obvious restraint.

'Certainly, Dr Balfour. Just as soon as I've seen my patient away.' That was a must. She was obviously about to get a rocket, and Mrs Turnbull was quite capable of listening at the door!

Having seen her off the premises and locked the

outside door behind her, Lindy hurried back to set the new man straight. 'Everything is quite in order, Doctor,' she began brightly, by way of defusing his wrath.

It wasn't enough. Lyall Balfour took a sharp breath before asking with barely controlled impatience, 'Does that mean you hadn't been using that short-wave diathermy machine?'

'No, Doctor, but——'

'No buts, please. Standing in for the receptionist—even doing a few basic nursing duties—is all very well, but I cannot sanction your giving electrotherapy. Apart from the dangers and the legal position, have you thought what your father would say?'

'My father knows—in fact it was his idea. You see——'

'I don't believe it!' he hissed, looking quite murderous.

'I can explain,' Lindy said in a small voice, wishing she'd done it sooner, instead of reinforcing his impression of her extreme youth with all those silly remarks. 'You see, with the hospital being so far away and so many of our patients so frail, and——' She was doing this all wrong. 'I think I'll start agin,' she whispered, almost silenced by the blackness of his scowl.

'Don't bother. There is no explanation which will excuse this—this irregularity. And if my partners are aware of what's being going on, then I'd rather not know. But there's to be no more of it, understand? I simply will not allow it!'

'Even if I were to tell you that I'm properly qualified?' asked Lindy timidly.

That didn't produce the lowering of the temperature she'd expected. Instead Lyall Balfour ran a distracted hand through his hair and said on a dying breath, 'I presume you're about to tell me you're taking a correspondence course.'

With his hair standing on end like that he didn't look nearly so awe-inspiring. 'I'm not going to tell you anything so unethical. I went to college in Edinburgh and got my BSc degree last summer. I'm also a member of the Chartered Society of Physiotherapy. And if that doesn't make me properly qualified, I don't know what will!'

As he had got so uptight at the idea of a quack in the fold, Lindy had fully expected a show of heartfelt relief, but if anything, he was now even angrier. 'Then why couldn't you have said so in the beginning,' he asked tightly, 'instead of pretending to be just an overgrown schoolgirl? What was the point? Apart from trying to make a fool of me?'

She was all ready to burst out with a torrent of self-defence, but she checked on hearing her father's step in the corridor. He would be very upset to hear her shouting and quarrelling with his new partner, no matter how justified she might be. 'You started it by talking down to me the way you did,' she said as quietly as her indignation would allow. 'How do you suppose I liked that? And if you're feeling foolish now, just imagine how I did before. I'd say we're now just about even!' And with that, she swept out and rushed into the house. She really ought to have tidied up her father's room first, but she wasn't risking Lyall Balfour coming too and flattening her with a few well-chosen words as she was pretty sure he would.

When her father came looking for his tea some time later, Lindy had calmed down, though not quite enough, it seemed, because he told her, 'You have a very expressive face, my child, so out with it. What's the matter?'

'Nothing — really,' she mumbled.

'I saw Lyall just now, and he also seems to be less than his usual collected self, so —— '

'All right, then — we've just had a row. No, not a row exactly,' she added when her father frowned. 'More of a — a . . .' she gave up trying to describe it. 'He came in and caught me switching off the diathermy machine and started to read the riot act. Of course I told him I'm properly qualified, and then he really went off the deep end and accused me of trying to make a fool of him by playing the schoolgirl. I told him he'd made me feel pretty foolish by treating me like one, so I reckoned we were just about quits. I'm sorry, Pa, but you may as well know it. He really gets up my nose.'

'I cannot see why, Lindsay, but I hope you'll manage to conceal that from now on.'

That was a command, not a hope. 'I'll not rock the boat if he doesn't,' Lindy returned mutinously. 'But I'm not as good as you are at believing the best of everybody.' She had to say it! 'Do you really not feel any doubts at all about him?'

'Such as?'

'Why here? Why us? Why not a smart private practice in the southern yuppie belt?'

'Can a man not get back to his roots without raising suspicions?' queried her father.

Lindy dismissed that with a wave of the hand. 'How much do you really know about him, Pa? Apart from his professional record, which I take it must be OK?'

'It's very much more than merely OK. And as Professor Stewart of St Crispin's Hospital Medical School has vouched for him in the most glowing terms both professionally and personally, that's quite good enough for me. Gordon Stewart and I shared digs throughout our student years, and there's no better way of getting to know a man than that.'

It was obvious that her woolly misgivings counted for nothing against a recommendation like that. And what, after all, did they amount to? Not a lot more than resentment because Lyall made her feel inadequate, homespun and naïve. And yet he was concealing *something*. She just knew it.

'Are you going to pour out, dear, or are we having iced tea with our scones today?' her father asked, reverting to his usual mildness and jerking Lindy out of her reverie.

'Sorry, Pa. Coming right up. And while we're on the subject of food, do you mind if we eat early tonight? Elspeth's called an extra meeting of the gang.'

To that her father said that he didn't mind a bit; she didn't get out nearly enough with folk her own age, and anyway, he'd half a mind to look in at the golf club later on. Everybody happy, then, so all Lindy had to do was her best to look at least half as smart as Elspeth for once.

But, walking into the lounge bar of the Eyretoun Arms later on that evening, Lindy realised that her friend had outdone her yet again. In a stunning trouser suit of subtle pink, she made Lindy feel quite dowdy in her neat green cotton skirt and blouse. And Elspeth was so thin too, with never a bulge up front or down back to mar the line. Lindy sighed. The only time she'd tried to diet away her own distinctly feminine curves, all she'd had to show for it were hollow cheeks and feet that slipped about in her shoes.

And why had she not tried to put them off coming here? It wasn't that Bill and Andy got drunk — just that a couple of pints made them even heartier than usual. And if cool, suave Lyall Balfour was to see her in such company. . . Lindy reined in her thoughts, aghast. It had come to something if he could prompt her to criticise her friends. Her greeting for them was warmer than usual as a consequence.

Bill took that for encouragement, and, slipping an arm round Lindy's waist, he teased, 'You're in a gey good mood tonight.'

'Does that mean I'm not usually?' she returned, dimpling.

'Och, I'd not say that—just that you seem to be even more cheerful than usual, that's all.'

'And that's nothing to do with your father's new partner, of course,' put in Elspeth, head on one side.

Lindy hated it when Elspeth took this line; she was just too damned good at it. 'Naturally I'm very relieved that Pa's got the extra help he's been needing so badly,' she returned firmly.

'Come off it!' laughed Elspeth. 'You'll never persuade me you've not noticed how gorgeous he is.' She sighed. 'Married, or at least spoken for, though, one supposes.'

Although nobody had actually said so, Lindy had got the impression that he wasn't, but debating the point with Elspeth was not the best way of shutting her up. 'More than likely—at his age,' she agreed. Then she turned to Andy, who had been frowning heavily ever since Elspeth called the new doctor gorgeous. 'So how's the car going now?' she asked.

Andy's scowl halved. When not playing rugby, he was usually on some car rally or other, to the despair of his father. 'Sweet as a nut, Lindy, since I —— ' He went off into a long and involved description of mechanical achievements which left his friends bewildered.

'Wonderful,' said Bill satirically when Andy paused for breath. 'Pity I can't do somthing similar to that old bull of your dad's. I'm tired of telling him it's time he was pensioned off.'

'The old man too. Now if only he'd retire —— '

'You'd turn the farm into a combination rugby pitch and racetrack,' said Elspeth. 'Did I tell you guys I've landed a huge great contract to sell in Japan?'

'Sell what? Woolly kimonos to geishas?' asked Bill with a grin.

Elspth thumped him, and then they were all away with the cheerful, quickfire exchanges that characterised all their evenings together. Outsiders like the new doctor were now forgotten.

But the bar was filling up quicker than usual tonight, with a crowd of tourists as well as the usual quota of locals. The atmosphere was smoky and the noise too great now for chat. When Elspeth suggested that they adjourn to her place, the idea was warmly applauded.

Lyall was coming up the hotel steps as they emerged. In one minute flat, Elspeth had made the introductions, told Lyall where they were going and invited him to join them. He readily agreed. On the short walk to her riverside home, Elspeth walked ahead with him, leaving Lindy following between a curious Bill and a tight-lipped Andy, responding as best she could to each, while marvelling at the way Elspeth was drawing Lyall out. He was answering her freely and laughing quite a lot. When he turned to Elspeth, which he did rather often, Lindy examined his handsome profile and felt betrayed. Her friend had no business to be getting on so well with him when she couldn't. If she could have thought of a plausible excuse, she'd have made it and gone home right then.

Elspeth had contrived some ultra-modern living space at one end of her mill. A spiral wrought-iron stair led up from a huge living-room to a galleried bedroom. Her high-tech open-plan kitchen occupied the space beneath. Asked for his opinion, Lyall was full of praise.

'I designed it myself,' revealed Elspeth then, her famous eyelashes working overtime.

'Really? If your knitwear is as original as this, I can see why you need to expand.'

Oh, *very* smooth! Elspeth must have been telling him about her new contract on the way here. How successful had she been at finding out things about him? 'I'll give you a hand, Elspeth,' Lindy decided firmly, stepping round Lyall and preceding Elspeth into the kitchen.

If she had already picked Lyall as her help, Elspeth was too sophisticaed to show disappointment. 'Bless you, girl,' she tinkled, while Lyall, thwarted, wandered off to join the boys at the other end of the room, where large chairs and couches were angled round an open fireplace.

With the men safely out of earshot, Lindy asked, 'Are you not taking a bit of a risk here? Andy's livid.'

'So what? He's been taking me much too much for granted lately. The possibility of a rival will do him good.'

'Then I hope Lyall will co-operate,' said Lindy, hoping nothing of the sort. She didn't want him muscling in and breaking up their cosy little group, now did she?

'He will,' predicted Elspeth confidently. 'He seemed rather reserved at first — though I can't think why, with all he's got going for him — but I'm already thawing him out. There are biscuits in this tin.' She slid it along the counter top, together with a quick bright glance. 'Not treading on you toes, am I?'

'Don't be silly!' retorted Lindy sharply.

'Only asking. After all, you get priority — his partner's daughter, and all that.'

'Don't be silly,' Lindy repeated in the absence of inspiration. 'Anyway, how do we know he hasn't got somebody down south?' But before Lindy could discover whether or not Elspeth knew more than she did, Bill came strolling across to ask how long it took to make a simple thing like a pot of coffee.

Elspeth glared and gave him the tray to carry for his punishment. Lindy followed them slowly and chose a chair well away from Lyall, where she could watch him unnoticed and listen to him geting on to good terms with her friends.

Bill was soon won over by an appeal to find Lyall a dog once he was settled in a house with a garden, and even Andy thawed out a bit on discovering that the Ferrari he'd admired parked outside the hotel actually belonged to the new doctor. As for Elspeth, sitting beside Lyall on he sofa, she could hardly keep her hands to herself.

So everybody meets with his approval except me, thought Lindy. What a thought! She was still mulling that over when Bill asked—and not for the first time, apparently, 'Are you coming home tonight, Lindy, girl, or have you taken root?'

'Sorry—I was nearly asleep. I've had a very tiring day,' she added loudly with an oblique glance for the main cause of it. He was much too busy saying a protracted goodnight and thank you to Elspeth to heed her, though.

Andy insisted on staying behind to wash the cups—something he'd never done before—and as Bill lived halfway between here and home that would leave Lindy and Lyall to go the last half-mile together. Lindy found that both a disturbing and a pleasing idea. How would he behave, and what would he say after their last highly unsatisactory exchange that afternoon? But, once in the High Street, it became clear that Bill meant to walk all the way home with her, instead of leaving her with a casual peck on the cheek at his own front door as he usually did. So they walked on, the two men chatting easily until Lyall left them outside the Eyretoun Arms with a friendly goodnight and hopes of a repeat evening some time.

'Nice guy,' considered Bill as they strolled across the town green towards Downside House.

'Charming,' returned Lindy with an irony that Bill missed entirely.

'All the same, you'll not be getting too friendly with him, I hope.'

'Would you not like that, Bill?'

'I certainly wouldn't advise it when Elspeth seems to have set her sights on him.'

And of course if Elspeth wants him, there's no chance for me! 'Thanks for the compliment, pal,' Lindy said wryly.

'Look here—I didn't mean. . .' Bill stuttered to a standstill. 'Anyway, you're much nicer than she is, you know. She's as hard as nails under all that glamour.'

Lindy would rather Bill had praised her looks than her personality. 'Poor old Andy,' she observed obliquely.

'He was never in with a chance—not while his father holds the purse strings,' Bill returned positively.

He was being positive all round tonight. Instead of the usual peck on the cheek, he took Lindy by the shoulders and kissed her firmly on the mouth. She'd been expecting him to do that for some time, and was disappointed to find it had left her entirely unmoved. 'Goodnight then, Lindy, pet,' he whispered. 'We must go out by ourselves some time.'

'That'll be nice,' she said. But would it? And what kind of an endearment was 'pet' from a man who spent half his time treating them?

'So I'll give you a ring about it, then, shall I?'

'That'll be nice.' She was repeating herself rather a lot

tonight. 'Goodnight then, Bill — and thanks for seeing me home.'

'My pleasure,' he said firmly, following up with another kiss which had no more effect on her than the first one. Then he walked away across the grass.

Lights were going out one by one in the windows of the hotel across the way. Which one was Lyall's?

CHAPTER THREE

'GOOD morning, Doctor.'

'Good morning, Lindy. Do we have a busy surgery this morning?'

'Fewer patients than yesterday. The records are already on your desk.'

'Thanks. Then may I have the first one in, please?'

'Of course. Mrs Marshall? Dr Balfour will see you now.' So far so good, and better than yesterday.

'Whaur's ma right doctor?' demanded the patient, ruffling the waters.

Lindy made sure that Lyall had closed the consulting-room door before saying on a whisper, 'You know my father's been ill, Mrs Marshall, and Dr Balfour is here to take over most of his work.

'They're saying your dad is still seeing some folk, though.'

'Yes—but he's wanting Dr Balfour's opinion of your case,' Lindy was inspired to say. And it was certainly an idea, when the new man was said to have special knowledge of her sort of problem.

'I'd rather see your father, Lindsay.'

But he's only taking two morning surgeries these days, Mrs Marshall. Oh, do please come, or Dr Balfour will be cross with me!'

'So whit does he think he is, then—the Pope?' growled the old lady, but she couldn't resist that pathetic plea, having always had a soft spot for the doctor's wee lassie.

With Lyall then safely shut up with his first case of the day, Lindy booked in he newest arrival before taking

Ellen her records. 'So how's it going this morning, Lindy?' asked Ellen.

'Better than yesterday, thank heaven.' Don't tempt fate. 'So far, that is.'

'He's a nice lad at bottom, you know.'

'I'm sure you're right, Ell.' At least, I hope you are! 'Are you ready for your first patient?'

'Give me two more secs, dear. I want to look something up.'

'Right you are. Now what on earth? 'Scuse me. . .' Lindy scuttled out as the bell at Reception pealed long and loud.

A middle-aged man in bright new leisure gear stood by the desk, tenderly cradling a damaged wrist, and Lindy had him down for a tourist even before hearing his southern accent. 'I'm ever so sorry to have to trouble you, miss,' he began, 'but I was changing a wheel and the jack broke.'

'What rotten luck,' she sympathised on seeing the telltale distortion of his wrist. 'Come and sit down while I take your particulars and then I'll get you seen as quickly as possible.'

It was a good thing that Lyall's next patient was late. Armed with a completed card, Lindy knocked on his door. 'Could I trouble you to see an emergency, Dr Balfour? It looks awfully like a Colles' fracture to me.' How daft could you get? Now he'd probably tick her off for exceeding her role.

He didn't. 'Does it, indeed? Then I dare say that's what it is.'

A tacit acknowledgment of her profesional expertise! 'Thank you, Doctor.'

A quick glance and Lyall confirmed her diagnosis. 'How unfortunate when you're on holiday, Mr Beccles,' he said, sounding genuinely sympathetic. 'I'm afraid it's definitely a fracture, so that means a visit to hospital. Miss Dunbar will arrange that — and also immobilise it to give you temporary relief.'

'You don't want to do that yourself, then?' Lindy couldn't believe it.'

'No — I'm sure you'll do an excellent job. Of course, if you're too busy. . .'

'Oh, no, I'm not. Thanks for trusting me, Doctor.'

He shrugged at that, making Lindy wish she'd kept that last remark to herself. Had he thought she was being sarcastic? Oh, stop analysing every damn thing he says, Lindsay Dunbar! You're far too aware of the wretched man.

'That feels much better,' said the patient when Lindy had splinted his wrist and put the arm in a sling. 'I do believe I could just —— '

'No, you cannot just leave it until you get home,' she insisted. 'There is obviously some displacement, and it'll have to be reduced and put in a plaster cast if it's not to cause you a lot of trouble in the future. I'm sorry, but our nearest hospital is over at Roxburgh. This part of the world is very sparsely populated, compared with yours. Now here's what you should do. . .'

When Lindy took Lyall his coffee and his list of visits, he was dictating into his fancy little gadget again. At this rate, poor Mrs Gavin would soon be having a nervous breakdown. He switched off at once and stood up. From courtesy, or a desire for mastery? He overtopped her by a good six inches. 'About that Colles' fracture,' he began.

'Splinted and probably at the hospital by now. I arranged for the local garage to fix his car, and fortunately his wife can take over the driving.'

'Well done!' There was a slight pause before he told her he was sending Mrs Marshall to see a consultant.

Lindy didn't know whether to be relieved or indignant because he had succeeded where her father had failed. 'You mean you've actually persuaded her?' He nodded. 'My father's been trying to get her to go for ages and she's always refused.'

'Sometimes — a new broom. . .'

'Quite!' She had put a whole world of meaning into that one word.

'And while you're here, I'd like to apologise for yesterday,' he said quietly. 'I should have realised you were a physio at once. Apart from anything else, your father would never have allowed anything so unethical.' He smiled crookedly. 'But in my own defence I have to say this. I've seen fifth-formers who look older that you do.'

Lindy was nothing if not fair. 'I knew that was what you thought, and I shouldn't have played along. It was — silly.'

This time he managed a full-scale smile. 'I'm very glad we've got that out of the way,' he said. 'It'll be much easier to work together now that we know where we stand.'

'That's right,' she agreed, but did they? She was still in the dark about his motives for coming to Eyretoun. 'But your coffee's getting cold,' she said just as the phone rang in reception. 'Excuse me, please.'

It was Bill. 'Oh, hello,' she said. 'What's your problem?'

'I don't have a problem. I just wondered if you were free to have dinner with me tonight. Just us — not the others.'

'That sounds very——' Lindy closed her mouth with a snap when Lyall came out of his room. 'I'm very sorry, but the evening list is full.'

'Have you gone bananas?' Bill asked faintly.

Lindy was wondering that herself. What did it matter if Lyall did overhear her making a date?

But Lyall had heard, and he stopped by the desk. 'Never mind about the list being full if that's an urgent case. Let me speak to the patient.'

Lindy leapt back as if stung and thrust the phone behind her back. 'It's not — it'll keep.'

'Let me be the judge of that,' he said, advancing purposefully and holding out his hand.

Instead of telling him the truth, Lindy handed over the phone, like the mesmerised idiot he seemed able to make of her.

'Dr Balfour here,' he said. 'What's the trouble?' Concern gave way to surprise and finally to amusement — damn him! 'Then why couldn't she have said so, instead of pretending? Had you finished your chat, Bill, or do you want to speak to her again?'

Bill must have said yes, please, because Lyall passed the wretched instrument back across the desk. 'N-no — it doesn't matter,' mumbled Lindy, now bright red with embarrassment.

With a wicked gleam in his eye, Lyall leaned across the desk, bringing his face close to hers. 'Now you don't just look like a schoolgirl, you're behaving like one too,' he whispered. Then he laid the phone down in front of her and went grinning on his way to Ellen's room.

'You're not scared of him, are you?' asked Bill when Lindy eventually managed to say, 'Hello again.'

'No, of course I'm not.' Yet in a funny kind of way I am, she realised unhappily.

'I must say I didn't really see how you could be. Anyway, I'll pick you up at six and we'll drive over to Kelso and try that new place. OK?'

'Lovely — and thanks, Bill. I'm sorry I was so silly.'

'Tell that to Lyall,' said Bill with a chuckle as he rang off.

When Lyall came out of Ellen's room, Lindy was sifting through a great pile of records. 'Still at it, I see,' he observed pleasantly.

'Yes,' she agreed without looking up. 'There's always such a lot of filing to be done.'

'More help is definitely needed.'

He could have meant that kindly, but Lindy was still smarting from their last humiliating encounter, so she took it for criticism. 'I can manage, Dr Balfour!'

He shrugged, giving up the attempt to be friendly. 'Just managing is not always enough,' he returned quietly before setting out on his rounds.

Lindy abandoned the filing then and went to talk to Ellen. She began by asking if her father had told his cousin about yesterday's stramash.

'You mean when Lyall came in and caught you giving SWD—illegally, as he thought?' cackled Ellen. 'What a laugh! I wish I'd been there. Sorry,' she added, sobering down when she noticed Lindy's wounded expression. 'You two just don't hit it off, do you? A case of chalk and cheese, I reckon. A pity, but it can't be helped, and there'll be no call for you to see much of one another when we've got a real nurse on the job. But I can't stand here gossiping all day—I've got visits to make.' Ellen grabbed her bag and dashed off, leaving Lindy thoughtful.

Ellen's reading of the situation was spot on—and very depressing. She'd also reminded Lindy that when Lyall's sister came—Lindy didn't doubt that she would—she herself would be out of a job. And then what would she do?

Meg was washing out her dusters when Lindy went into the house. 'Look at that!' she exclaimed excitedly, pointing to the table on which lay an enormous spray of flowers beautifully done up in cellophane and ribbon. 'That Dr Balfour is a lovely man.' No wonder Meg thought that if he'd sent her these for just a three-day stay! And she'd obviously quite forgiven his inadequate attempts at bath-cleaning.

'Your dad got golf balls and a bottle of brandy and I got chocolates,' Meg continued. 'And I never even saw him to speak to! Now that's what I call a real gentleman.'

So the flowers must be for me, then, realised Lindy. Now she was feeling almost as excited as Meg. She opened the card and read — 'Thank you for making me feel so welcome and comfortable.' Talk about coals of fire! Her pleasure evaporated. She hadn't really done either. Now if only she could put the clock back to Friday and start again. . . She couldn't, but she could thank him nicely the next time she saw him, and also try hard not to disagree with him any more.

Lindy hadn't anybody coming for treatment that afternoon, but as she had to be on standby for incoming messages, she thought she might as well tackle some of the paperwork. She'd been at it for almost an hour and was congratulating herself on the rare tidiness of the tiny office when the phone rang. The second she lifted it a child's voice said breathlessly, 'We're needin' the doctor right away — now! Ma dad's —— '

'Address, please,' Lindy broke in firmly. Agitated callers had been known to ring off before giving that vital bit of information.

'Muirhead Farm.' Right on Lyall's route. 'Ma dad's havin' a heart attack!'

Lindy had recognised the voice now. 'All right, Bobby, Doctor will be there as soon as possible. What sort of pain is it?'

'It's awful bad. Ma mammy says to hurry——' Click. Bobby had rung off.

Lindy checked Lyall's list, then rang the Anderson place to be told she'd just missed him. Damn! Either he was being very quick, or he was visiting out of the sequence she'd worked out so carefully, to save time and backtracking.

Dial again. Good! Not yet at the Guthries'. Lindy left a message for him to hurry to Muirhead Farm as fast as he could. She'd done her best, but worried still. It was no use trying to contact either of the other doctors, with her father away in quite the opposite direction and Ellen heaven knew where on her half day. But if old man Carswell was really having a heart attck, he'd need to go to hospital. Lindy dialled 999 for an ambulance. Then she rang all the other patients on Lyall's list on the off chance of catching him. Then, confident of having done all she could, she went back to her paperwork.

Both duty doctors arrived back at base within minutes of each other. Lindy had already made tea for her father, but on hearing the surgery door slam, she took some to Lyall. It would be a good chance to thank him for the flowers.

She found him in Pa's consulting-room—as she still thought of it—on the phone, and apologising to somebody. She waited until she heard the closing ping before taking in the tray. 'I thought you might like some tea, Doctor,' she told him.

'Thank you—that was very thoughtful.' But he didn't sound grateful; he sounded very, very cross.

'That's—all right.' She'd got the length of the door before he asked stiltedly, 'Don't you want to know the outcome of the Carswell affair?'

She turned and saw him regarding her gravely. She

knew she'd done her very best, but she felt a stab of fear all the same. 'Were you — in time?'

'I was.'

'Thank goodness for that! Did he need to go to hospital?'

'No.' Did he have to be quite so terse?

'You mean — it wasn't a heart attack after all?'

'No. Just a severe attack of indigestion.'

'All's well that ends well, then,' she concluded fatuously.

'As it happens, yes. But it might have been different if the man really had sustained a myocardial infarct.'

He was definitely leading up to something, but what could it be? 'No blame attached to us, though,' Lindy insisted. 'We couldn't possibly have responded quicker.' *I* couldn't anyway. *You* could if you'd stuck to the route plan I gave you. . .

'You're very complacent,' he said quietly. 'Are you really that sure?'

'*I'm* complacent!' Lindy was ready to lose her temper now. 'I know this district. I know within minutes how long it takes to get from place to place. So I gave you the best route — and you didn't stick to it. If you had, I could have contacted you sooner. Anyway, I was the one who contacted the ambulance station.'

'I know — and I've apologised for the waste of their time,' Lyall assured her.

'It's very easy to be wise — after the event.'

'How true. But it's better to be wise before.'

'All right — let's have it,' she snarled. 'You obviously think I've made a mess of the whole thing, but as I can't see how, you'll have to tell me!'

He folded his arms across his perfectly tailored jacket. 'Why didn't you call me direct?'

'I tried to, but you were out of range,' Lindy explained.

'By bleep, yes — but not on the car-phone.'

'Car-phone! How the hell was I supposed to know you've got a car-phone?'

He frowned down his nose, infuriating her further. 'The number's on the card pinned up at Reception.'

'I — thought that was the hotel. I mean, hotels do often have more than one number. . . You should have told me!' she finished on a stronger note.

'Obviously.'

Suddenly Lindy realised she'd had enough of his particular brand of restrained disapproval. Correction — more than enough. And this time her father wasn't around to be considered. 'You think I'm disorganised, inefficient and stupid, and you've made that very clear. And it doesn't bother me —' what a lie! '—— because I don't like you either. You're too darned superior by half — so there!' Having relieved herself of her resentment, Lindy glared at him, cheeks flushed and bosom heaving.

He stared just as steadily back as he said deliberately, 'While making every possible allowance for the fact that you're doing a job for which you've had no training, I must reserve the right to point out your mistakes — especially when a life could be at stake. And that's all I was doing.'

'So you don't think you could be partly to blame for not telling me you have a car-phone?'

'In my experience, physiotherapists are intelligent people who don't need everything that's written down spelled out for them as well.'

In other words, she was not only completely in the wrong, she was also unfit to be a physio! 'I don't accept that,' she said, too angry to care that her meaning wasn't crystal clear. 'Now then, are you going to tell my father about my — my utter incompetence and stupidity, or shall I?'

'I don't see why he has to be bothered with this. He's got quite enough to worry about already.'

'Such as having *me* for a daughter, no doubt!' snapped Lindy.

'Now you're being absurd,' he said, reverting to his adult-to-adolescent tone again. And so damned cool with it! How did he manage it?

'You're impossible!' she stormed. 'You can't even lose your temper like a normal human being. Have you no feelings at all?'

That final shaft went straight to the target, and for one brief second his face was distorted by a spasm of pain, before he answered with the same iron control as before. 'I'd always thought that the ability to keep one's temper was a sign of maturity,' he said icily.

Lindy gasped, shuddered and fled. She couldn't rejoin her father in the house after that. She needed to be alone with her shame. What was it about the man that provoked her to behave so childishly? She couldn't think of that scene without wanting to cry, and he had controlled himself so well. And this self-disgust wasn't the worst of it. How shocked and appalled her father would be if he knew!

Poor Lindy was still brooding hours later when she heard Bill's car in the drive. Feeling guilty about that scene in the surgery, she had cooked her father a more than usually delicious dinner. But preparing it had taken time, and she'd been obliged to hurry over bathing and dressing.

'You've had a helluva day,' said Bill when she joined him on the doorstep.

'How do you kow that?' she asked with a pathetic attempt at a smile.

'For one thing, you're wearing earrings that don't match.'

'Damn!' Lindy yanked them off and thrust them into her bag.

'Do you want to talk about it?' askd Bill as they set off.

What she would have loved to do was to tell all exactly as it happened and then hear Bill say she'd been absolutely right; the new partner was indeed an uptight, fault-finding bully. But she knew just fine that the situation wasn't that clear-cut. 'I just can't seem to get on to Lyall Balfour's wavelength,' she said eventually with wonderful understatement.

'These things are usually mutual, so I dare say he feels the same,' observed Bill, getting nearer the truth than he could know. And giving Lindy no comfort at all. 'Don't let it worry you, though, or you'll get it all out of proportion.'

'He disapproves of everything I do—so of course I keep on making mistakes,' she exaggerated, wanting sympathy.

'Are you sure you're not overreacting?'

'Positive!'

'Keep out of his way as much as possible, then,' advised Bill. Good advice, but hard to follow in present circumstances. Lindy opened her mouth to tell him so just as he added, 'And don't dwell on it, either. Forget the problem when you have the chance. Like now, for instance.'

She took the hint. Bill wasn't taking her out to dinner at great expense in order to listen to her going on about her differences with another man. So Lindy did her best to be good company, but try as she would, she couldn't forget the afternoon's humiliation. She was abstracted all evening, so it was no surprise when Bill told her she was looking tired, before taking her the short way home without stopping. For that, Lindy was grateful, though it would have been a disappointment before Lyall Balfour came.

The house was in darkness except for the light over the front door, so Pa must be out. Rather than go in and brood some more, Lindy decided on a stroll around the green in the balmy spring darkness. She tried to think positively. Somehow she must learn to keep calm and guard against mistakes. Then there'd be no reason for reproofs.

She was so deep in thought that she almost bumped into the object of her preoccupation, who was also taking a stroll before turning in. He had to side-step smartly to avoid her. 'Are you all right?' he asked in his detached, doctor's voice.

'Yes, thank you. I'm fine.' But she wasn't. 'No, I am not,' she breathed. 'I've gone over and over it—and I'm still not sure that muddle this afternoon was all my fault. I've been wretched ever since, all the same. I'm not usually stupid, you know—I don't know why, but you make me. . .thoroughly nervous!'

'*Do* I?' He sounded absolutely incredulous. 'Nobody has ever told me that before.'

'I expect that's because you're so—so self-possessed and remote that nobody ever dared.' Oh, God, this tongue of hers! She was making things worse, not better. 'Forget I said that—please!' she begged.

'I'll try if it's that important, but it won't be easy.'

'And you sent those beautiful flowers!' she wailed, suddenly remembering. 'They're lovely—quite lovely. Such a pity that I don't deserve them!' Her voice broke on a sob. She turned away desolate, and ran as fleet as a hare across the grass towards home, heedless when he called after her.

Lyall stood motionless in thought for quite a while before he went back to the hotel.

CHAPTER FOUR

MEG had left the kitchen window open again and a thin film of dust covered everything. Lindy slammed it shut, muffling the noise the builders were making. Then she took a damp cloth to the table and worktops. The shell of the new surgery extension was now in place and work had started on the interior. In another few weeks it would be ready.

When the idea had first been discussed, Lindy had expected Christmas to come and go before they got this far. Look how long it had taken to get planning permission when Pa had extended the waiting-room some years back. But she had reckoned without Lyall Balfour's energy and skill at cutting through the red tape.

She had also worried about the cost, only to discover that Lyall was putting up the money. Inevitably she had wanted to know why, to which her father had answered that, as he and Ellen would be retiring in the next few years, the long-term benefit would all be Lyall's. So he had insisted on shouldering the cost.

Generosity like that was bound to weaken suspicion and resentment — especially when coupled with the kind of kid-glove courtesy he'd been showing her ever since their late-night encounter on the town green all those weeks ago. The trouble was that such treatment stifled her natural spontaneity. It was difficult to get on to relaxed and friendly terms with somebody who treated you as carefully as he would a time-bomb. Once or twice, she'd thought she'd cracked it, but next day they were always back to square one.

There was one consolation. Elspeth wasn't making much headway either. Or rather, not the sort she had in mind. Despite engineering a couple of candlelight dinners at her place and some cultural excursions to Edinburgh, she hadn't yet managed to get Lyall into bed. 'Perhaps he doesn't—you know—like women,' Lindy had suggested, wondering why that idea should cause her such a pang.

Elspeth had pooh-poohed that for an idea, and with all her experience, she should know. Lindy had felt a bit better after that.

'What's for lunch today, dear?' asked her father, coming in just then.

Nothing if I don't get a move on, thought Lindy, coming out of her reverie with a start. 'Soup and salad in about ten minutes?'

'Enough for three, do you think?'

'Sure, Pa. Ellen doesn't eat much.'

'Actually, it's Lyall I've asked to join us today,' he returned casually, strolling over to the window. 'Is it not just great the way he's got things moving?'

'Yes—marvellous.' Have the chicken cold now, instead of currying it for supper. . .

'We'll be able to offer a much better service when it's up and running.' Her father sighed. 'I should have done this years ago, but somehow—with losing your mother and so on—I just hadn't the heart.'

'You worked yourself to a standstill, so I don't know what more you think you could have done,' Lindy protested warmly. 'And surely it's the quality of the work that counts, not the building it's done in,' she added earnestly.

'I hope you don't mind me asking Lyall to lunch, dear, only we were expecting the architect to come this morning and he didn't show up. He might come yet, so as Lyall needs to be on the spot. . .'

'Of course I don't mind, Pa. Why would I?' And don't tell me it's because I'm never myself with him — I know that! 'We'll need to eat in here, though. Meg's got the dining-room upside-down.'

'I'll bring the sherry through, then,' said her father.

Sherry — in the middle of the day? Anybody would think there was something to celebrate, Lindy was thinking when Lyall appeared. 'I'm afraid this must be a bit of an imposition,' he said carefully.

'Not in the least,' she insisted as she poured salad dressing over a bowl of greenery. 'Just pot luck, though.' She began to toss the salad.

'Your pot luck looks very superior to me,' Lyall assured her.

'You've always been very kind about my catering.'

'But not in other directions?'

Lindy made herself meet his steady gaze unblinking. 'I didn't say that — and I wasn't thinking it. In fact —' go on, quick before Pa comes back '—— I've been wanting to thank you for ages for what you've done for my father. He's so much better since you changed his medication and took all the admin. off his shoulders. I'm very grateful.' What a change! In the beginning, she'd seen all that as meddling.

'Thank you,' he said simply, but his smile was warmer than she'd seen it for some time.

Her father returned with the sherry, and the unaccustomed midday drink had Lindy sitting down to her lunch feeling quite mellow. 'Your sister will be in a great flurry of last-minute packing today,' she assumed chattily as she handed Lyall his soup. Deborah Balfour had gone along with her brother's suggestion and was arriving tomorrow.

'She has been for the past fortnight,' he answered. 'As well as packing up her own things, she's had the bother of deciding what furniture and stuff we'll need for the flat.' With faultless timing, the tenants of the best flat for rent in the town had moved out, and Lyall had taken it over.

Dr Dunbar asked when the furniture was expected.

'The day after Debbie — traffic permitting.'

'Two of my patients can't manage to come on Wednesday, so I could probably give her a hand,' offered Lindy, earning herself an approving glance from her father.

'That's extremely kind of you,' said Lyall, sounding astonished. As his sister would be putting Lindy out of work, it could be he'd expected hostility, not help.

'Don't give yourself indigestion, dear,' begged her father when Lindy hurried over to the dresser to get the second course.

'I have to hurry, Pa. I've got six patients coming for physio this afternoon, would you believe?' Her cheerful expression clouded over. 'It's not going to be easy breaking the news when I have to stop this.' Which couldn't be long now. With three doctors and only two consulting rooms, it was getting harder and harder to fit everything in.

'Who said anything about stopping?' asked her father, smiling.

'Nobody needs to, Pa. I know fine this can't go on.' And there was no possibility of work at the local hospital for the foreseeable future, yet how could she go back to Edinburgh before Pa was completely recovered?

The two doctors exchanged glances and Lyall drew a folded sheet of paper from his inside pocket. 'Read that,' he told her.

Lindy had to read it twice before she took it in. 'So

that's what that big room at the end of the new corridor is for,' she said slowly at last. 'A community physio based in the surgery is a wonderful idea — every general practice should have one.'

'Now what?' asked Lyall, who had been expecting an explosion of delight, not just muted approval.

'I do hope that somebody local gets the post — then that would mean a vacancy at the hospital.' For me! thought Lindy.

'Somebody local *is* getting it,' said Lyall. 'You are — if you want it. We're reserving the right to choose. No say in the appointment — no room available. Naturally they agreed.'

'Of course — when offered free premises,' added her father.

'Quite apart from all the money they'll save transporting patients to hospital, or sending a physio to treat them at home,' finished Lyall. 'But of course, if you're not interested. . .' He let that lie.

'I am — I am! But are you sure? I mean — will I do? I've not been qualified two years yet. You've got to be practical.' What she really wanted to know was whether he'd only agreed under pressure from her father.

'You'll be on the community superintendent physio's staff,' said Lyall, 'so you can get advice any time you need it. He's happy about the arrangement, so I don't see why you shouldn't be.'

'In that case. . .'

'I think it's time we drank a toast,' he said firmly.

After that Lindy had reluctantly to break up the party, because her patients would soon be arriving.

Mrs Gifford was first. Despite her initial misgivings, Lindy had cured her back pain, and so delighted was she that now she was having her arthritic shoulder loosened up. 'So how are things today, Mrs Gifford?'

'Not much different, dear, but then this is only my third visit, and it's been troublesome for ages.' Hadn't Lindy said something very like that about her back?

Mrs Rennie was still soldiering on without much improvement. If only I could have helped her, thought Lindy. Her turn had come for admission to hospital, and, while a neighbour had been willing to keep an eye on her husband, nobody had felt equal to coping with her retarded son. Being dead against him going into care, Mrs Rennie had let her chance go by.

The next two patients were farm workers, injured by a tractor in the same accident. Lindy enjoyed their visits because the banter between them was better than a play. 'So how's the ankle, Mr Meikle?' she began.

'Better than Tam's knee, m'lass. But then that wasnae straight to begin with.'

'It was so, Charlie Meikle. You're the one that hirpled about like the boss's old mare, and her with the arthritis since she fell o'er yon dyke.'

'Better an ol' mare than a thrawn old bull.'

'I think you two are more like a couple of chattering magpies,' said Lindy when she got the chance. You should save your breath for all the strenuous muscle building exercises I've got lined up for you today.'

Little Fiona Duffus had started coming for treatment every day on her way home from primary school. She had that distressing hereditary disease cystic fibrosis, in which fibrous lesions interfered with the functioning of the lungs and digestive system. She was a heroine, and considered herself lucky that only her lungs were affected. So she bore without complaint all the chest-clapping and rib vibration needed to clear her little lungs of the copious, sticky secretions which were such a weakening symptom.

'My, but you're coughing up a lot today, Fiona,' said Lindy gently.

'So I am, but my mammy didn't have time to shift much this morning. My wee brother was sick all over his bed.'

Calum, at four, also had cystic fibrosis, and Mrs Duffus's task could only get harder as time went on. I must ask Ellen if I should take him on too, Lindy was thinking. 'How does your mummy manage you both, Fiona?'

'The evenings is fine. Ma dad's home from his work and they take one each. He's getting awful good at the therapy,' Fiona added with the air of an expert, which in fact she was after years in and out of the children's hospital in Glasgow. The family had only recently moved back to Eyretoun after Mr Duffus was made redundant from his job in the shipyards.

'No more tummyaches, Fiona?'

'Och, no — I'm not so bad as Calum. He's a puir wee soul and ma granny says he'll not make old bones.'

Does she indeed? Then I'll be giving her a piece of my mind for saying such things in your hearing the next time I see her, Lindy decided grimly. 'How about one last go lying on your tummy over the pillows, sweetie? I've got a feeling there's still something lurking at the bottom of this right lung.'

'Aye, the posterior basal segment was aye the worst,' agreed the child. To know so much and be so philosophical at nine years old! Lindy could have wept.

'Thanks, miss. That's been a great help,' Fiona said politely when the session was over. She climbed off the plinth and picked up her schoolbag, buckling under the weight.

Lindy took it from her. 'Heavens, sweetie, this is far too heavy for you. I'll bring it up to the house later when

I've finished my work.' Lindy was strapping it to the carrier of her cycle when Lyall's car turned in at the gates.

'Is he a patient?' asked Fiona, gazing at the car.

'No, that's our new doctor.'

'What a smashing car, miss! I've never seen such a smashing car,' Fiona repeated as Lyall got out.

'Is this young lady a customer of ours?' he asked, giving Fiona a warm and gentle smile.

'Yes, this is Fiona Duffus,' explained Lindy. 'She comes for chest physio.'

''Cos I've got cystic fibrosis. Pleased to meet you, Doctor,' said Fiona, holding out a grubby little paw.

Lyall squatted down on his heel to shake hands. 'Charmed, I'm sure, Miss Fiona.'

Fiona giggled. 'You're a nice man,' she decided.

'And you're a very nice little girl. So you like my car, do you?'

'I think it's smashing.'

'Tell you what — I'll drive you home if you like.'

Fiona's eyes grew round with wonder. 'Ooh, Doctor, will you really?'

'It'll be a pleasure,' he assured her, opening the passenger door with a bow.

Mrs Turnbull arrived just as they were driving away. 'Where's he going with that child?' she demanded of Lindy.

'Her treatment exhausts her, so Dr Balfour is taking her home,' said Lindy, concocting a nice reply from two different facts. She led the way into the surgery.

'Mine exhausts me, but I don't notice anybody offering to take me home,' moaned the postmistress.

'How are you today?' asked Lindy, refusing to be drawn.

Her neck and shoulders were better, it seemed, but

her feet were slowly killing her. So far, though, her tongue and her curiosity were A1. 'Is that right your new doctor's a millionaire?' she demanded.

'Your guess is as good as mine, Mrs Turnbull.' If not better! 'Shoes and stockings off, now. And do you not think you'd be a lot more comfortable in flat lace-ups that didn't throw your weight forward?'

'Never could abide flat shoes,' said the patient. 'They're saying that extension of yours is costing a quarter of a million, and he's paying for it himself.'

'Imagine that!' said Lindy. 'But the financial side of things is not my concern. What did the orthopaedic surgeon say when you went to clinic?'

'You mean about my feet? It seems I'm needing Hellman's operations on my big toe joints.'

'Hellman's is mayonnaise, Mrs Turnbull. I think you must mean Keller's operation to straighten your big toes and cure your bunions.

'Aye, that sounds about right,' Mrs Turnbull agreed.

'You'll have to wear flat shoes after your operation, so you may as well get used to them now.'

'Sufficient unto the day is the evil thereof,' declared the patient, coming over quite biblical. 'Would you say it's wrong, then—what they're saying about Dr Balfour?'

'You'd better ask him yourself,' suggested Lindy, wishing she'd thought of that gossip-stifler before. 'Now then! Not all your walking difficulties are to do with your bunions, so I'm going to give you some electrical treatment to pep up your fallen arches.'

Just as Mrs Turnbull was leaving, Mrs Duffus rang up about Fiona's schoolbag. 'How silly I am!' exclaimed Lindy. 'I should have sent it with Dr Balfour. I'll cycle up with it this minute.'

Of course they spent some time discussing Fiona's progress, and when Lindy got home she found that her father had made the tea. 'Somebody's feeling better,' she teased.

'Somebody's got to get used to taking his full share of the chores for when his daughter's working a full day,' said her father. 'Are you pleased about the job, Lindy?'

'What do you think, Pa? Just as long as everybody is in favour.'

'Everybody is,' he insisted, knowing exactly what lay behind her proviso. 'Now do let's have our tea. I've got a lot of patients to be seen tonight.'

That set Lindy lecturing him on the dangers of overdoing things, a lecture from which he was glad to escape as soon as he could. He must be feeling better — he's beginning to rebel, decided his devoted daughter.

Well after midnight, Lindy was roused by a resounding crash that seemed to shake the house. It was followed soon after, and before she was fully awake, by somebody ringing the bell and hammering on the door. There was a lot of confused shouting going on somewhere close at hand. An accident, Lindy guessed as she dragged on the first pair of trousers that came to hand. She ran downstairs, struggling into a sweater as she went.

The girl on the step was too distraught to do more than sob a plea for help as she pointed a shaking finger towards the Green. By now, Dr Dunbar had come downstairs, bringing his black bag with him. Together they helped the girl down the drive.

Despite the late hour, a small crowd had gathered round a car which had crashed and concertinaed against one of the massive elm trees which ringed the town green. The doctor sent the nearest man for the police and another back into his own house to phone for the emergency services. Then he pushed through the throng to the wreck. He shone his torch into the car. 'God, what a mess,' he muttered. 'Fetch more supplies, Lindy — quick!'

She streaked back to the house and filled a carrier bag with dressings, bandages, splints, antiseptic and all the morphine she could lay her hands on. Then, grabbing as many blankets as she could carry, she ran back, praying that things weren't actually as bad as they seemed.

By then Lyall had arrived, roused by the noise of the crash. The police were there too.

The driver and the girl beside him were trapped, so apart from pain-killing injections nothing could be done for them until the fire brigade arrived to cut them free.

'Now let's see what else we've got,' Lyall said grimly, turning his attention to the back-seat passengers.

What they had got was a boy with a bad compound, comminuted fracture of tibia, a very dazed girl with a lacerated scalp, another boy with numerous cuts and bruises and the shocked girl who had raised the alarm. They were all in the mid-teens, and the smell of alcohol was very strong.

'Under age, drunk and the car stolen, I'm thinking,' rumbled a burly constable. 'They're all needin' locking up!'

'First things first, Jock, there'll be plenty of time for that,' retorted Lyall crisply. 'Lindy, come and help me splint this leg.'

'He's bearing this very well,' Lindy commented when they were nearly finished.

'Your father gave him an injection.' He squinted over his shoulder. 'What about that head injury, John?'

'The actual scalp wound is nothing, but she's badly concussed and almost certainly has a skull fracture.'

'That's four for hospital, then. Now for the last pair.'

'I don't know the others, but these two are locals,' said Lindy.

'Then we'll patch them up in the surgery and send them home,' Lyall was saying as a fire engine and two ambulances arrived.

'All this trouble! Weans their age should be home in their beds,' muttered the constable.

'You're absolutely right,' Dr Dunbar agreed peaceably. 'But if this doesn't teach them to mend their ways, then nothing can. We're taking these two up to the surgery now, and if you take my advice you'll wait for morning before questioning them.'

But the constable couldn't go along with that, and he plodded after the little party, intent on playing his part in the drama the minute the doctors had done.

Lyall stayed behind to brief the ambulance crews, and by the time he rejoined them, Lindy and her father had the boy on the plinth in the little dressing-room. He had an extensive, deep and jagged flesh wound over one shoulder that was going to need some skilful layer stitching. 'Heavens, Pa!' gasped Lindy when she uncovered that. 'Will I run down and tell them there's another one for the hospital?'

'Lyall will fix it,' said her father confidently, going to the drugs cupboard for some local anaesthetic.

At that point the girl passenger wandered in, saw the boy's wound and began to scream.

'I thought you were keeping an eye on her, Jock,' said Dr Dunbar reproachfully to the policeman.

'I was, Doctor, but she sort of wriggled away——'

Lyall arrived and seized the girl by the shoulders. He fixed her with a piercing look and hissed, 'Sit down and be quiet!' in a hypnotic voice. Then he pressed her into a chair and told Lindy to give her ten milligrams of valium in tablet form, before ringing her parents to come and collect her. Then he cast an eye over the boy's spectacular wound. 'That looks interesting,' he observed matter-of-factly.

He's had plenty of casualty experience, realised Lindy, as she gazed wide-eyed at the capable, cool-headed man who was Lyall Balfour under pressure.

When she came back from phoning, her father was leaning against the wall looking exhausted and Lyall was trying to persuade him to go back to bed. 'I can manage perfectly well, John.'

'I know that, lad, but you'll still need an assistant.'

'Lindy can help me.'

'She's not a nurse.'

'All she has to do is hand me things. Tell him, Lindy.'

'Lyall's right, Pa. You must go to bed. You've got early surgery tomorrow, remember.'

Her father opened his mouth to argue some more, read their determination and thought better of it.

Lyall then went back to collecting what he needed for the repair job, talking quietly to the boy all the time, explaining what he was going to do. 'Just as soon as the local anaesthetic takes full effect,' he ended. He looked across the bench at Lindy. 'You'd better start scrubbing — and make a thorough job of it.'

'Yes, Doctor.' When she had finished, Lyall took her place at the sink. He had removed his sweater and rolled up his shirt sleeves, revealing strong, well-muscled forearms. And more than that. On the front of his right wrist and forearm was an intricate criss-crossing of fine white scars which bespoke extensive damage and skilful, high-tech surgery. So Lyall Balfour was no stranger to injury himelf.

With the greatest difficulty, Lindy dragged her eyes away from those dreadful scars and went to talk to the boy, while swabbing him liberally with antiseptic all round his wound. Then she draped him with sterile towels, leaving only the wound exposed. She'd even managed to get a weak smile from him by the time Lyall was ready.

'Splendid,' he said approvingly. 'Where did you learn that?'

'Oh, here and there — by keeping my eyes open,' she answered.

'Very well observed.' He tested the skin around the wound with sharp-pointed scissors, ensuring complete loss of sensation before setting to work.

It was a painstaking and intricate job, resecting torn tissue, realigning structures — no nerve, tendon or major vascular damage, thank heaven — then closing layers of connective tissue before neatly suturing the skin. And all with such precision and skill. Lyall was obviously an experienced surgeon.

For the nth time, Lindy was asking herself why with skills like that he should have opted for general practice.

The constable had been watching from the doorway. 'Can he go home now, Doctor?' he asked as Lyall straightened up. 'His father's here with a car.'

Lyall was frowning and massaging his right forearm. 'Yes — but no lectures tonight, please.' He crossed to the drugs cupboard and counted some capsules into a bottle. He seemed to be having the greatest difficulty in writing directions on the label. 'For the pain,' he said to the boy. 'One when you get home and one four-hourly if you need it — but no more! I'll be counting when I visit you tomorrow morning.' He smiled tiredly. 'Are you all right now, lad?'

'Aye — and thanks, Doc. I never felt a thing.' Now the boy's lids were drooping as shock, fatigue and drugs got the better of him. His father, a big construction worker, scooped him up as though he were a baby and carried him out to the car. Lyall went with them, still issuing instructions.

While all that was going on, Lindy was clearing up the mess. She'd almost finished by the time Lyall returned. He was rubbing that arm again, and a discreet look told her the muscles were in spasm. He would probably bite her head off, but she had to try. 'Sit down,' she said gently. 'I can make a better job of that than you can.'

He obeyed her without a word, watching in silence as she slid a pillow between his arm and the table, before she stroked, kneaded and coaxed the tortured muscles to relax. 'Is it—all right now?' she asked at last on a whisper. Because only a whisper would do in the curiously intimate atmosphere of that little room, at three in the morning and with the old house silent and sleeping around them.

'As right as it ever is these days,' he whispered back.

'I'm so glad,' she returned simply, pulling down his sleeve and buttoning the cuff as she would for any patient.

He covered her hands with his free one. 'Don't you want to know what happened?'

'Only if you want to tell me,' she breathed gently, scared of breaking the spell. Hardly aware of doing so, she sank on to her elbows, coming closer.

Lyall was staring into space, his expression thoughtful. 'How many times have you heard a patient say "I walked into a door"?' he began. 'Well, that's exactly what I did. I was with—someone—who let it swing back right in my face, and I instinctively put out a hand, as one does. It couldn't have been very good glass, because it shattered—and with results you can guess at. I was out of action for months, and even now, nearly a year later, I can only just about manage twenty minutes of fine precision work — as you just saw.'

Brief, unemotional as it was, his account had explained much. Why he had taken two days to drive up from London. Why his golf clubs had remained in the boot of his car since the day he arrived. His manner, often so cool and remote, had been merely a mask for his disappointment. Because Lyall had been well up the surgical ladder. She was sure of it.

She allowed her cheek to brush ever so lightly across the top of his head before saying gently, 'Well, now you know where to come for treatment if you ever need it again. All very — private and professional.' Which was her way of telling him she would keep his secret.

He understood, and told her he did by the pressure of his grasp on her hands. 'You're a very special person, Lindy,' he said huskily. 'I've never known anyone quite like you.'

'That's a very wonderful thing to be told,' she whispered.

He looked at her directly for the first time since they had begun to talk. They stared into each other's eyes for seconds before he raised his hand slowly as though in a dream, cupping her chin and drawing her towards him. Their lips met softly, unhurriedly, but only once, before Lyall came out of that trance and got to his feet with a suddenness that startled and hurt her. 'I'm thoughtless — and selfish. Burdening you with my troubles when you must be utterly exhausted.'

His words and tone were gentle enough, but he was miles away from her now, the spell broken and the magic gone. Lindy could only stare at him, her eyes dark with disappointment.

A slow, tortured smile spread over his face as he bent to kiss her cheek. 'I'll never forget your kindness and understanding tonight,' he said. 'Now off to bed with you. I'll lock up here before I go.'

Bewildered and unhappy, Lindy did as she was told. Lyall had just written 'finish' to something she had thought was a new and wonderful beginning. Why?

CHAPTER FIVE

LINDY was stifling a full-scale yawn when Lyall walked into Reception next morning. 'Careful — you'll start me off,' he warned. 'That was some night, wasn't it?'

'You can say that again,' she responded lightly, tuning in to his wavelength. 'I had to wake my father this morning — for about the first time ever.'

'It's a pity this is one of his mornings for Surgery,' he went on with a frown. 'You'd better divert as many patients my way as you can.'

'I'd half thought of doing that anyway,' she confessed.

'How nice to find ourselves thinking alike,' he returned with the ghost of a smile before going into the consulting-room. A moment later he was on the phone.

Lindy had wondered how he would react after the quiet intimacy they'd shared in the aftermath of the accident. Now she knew. Friendly, certainly, but that was all. So she'd not been wrong when she sensed a drawing back after he had kissed her. That kiss had surprised him as much as her — and pleased him less!

When Lyall pressed the bell, Lindy ushered in his first patient. There was no chance of his falling asleep with Mrs Fraser in the room. She was stone deaf and thought that everybody else was too. Soon all the patients in the waiting-room knew that she had recently had an operation to release tight flexor tendons in the palm of her hand and would now be having lanolin massage to the operation scar to keep it supple, as well as exercises to increase movement and muscle strength.

'Good job she's no' had one of those special women's

ops, I'm thinking,' summed up the couthy wee body who kept the Bonny Scotland Gift shop. 'She'd no' be wantin' us to ken all aboot that. Is it my turn the noo?' she asked as Mrs Fraser reappeared.

'That's right — in you go, Miss Govan,' agreed Lindy. 'Can you come back for treatment this afternoon at two?' she screeched when Mrs Fraser presented her slip of paper.

'Twice in the one day? Why can I not get it now?' the patient bawled back as fiercely.

'There's no room *free!*' yelled Lindy, shaking her head as well for reinforcement.

'I should just hope it is free,' observed the patient at the top of her voice. 'I pay my taxes. I'll do this for you, though. I'll go and get my messages and maybe a nice cuppa at the Waverley Café — and come back about eleven.'

'Make it half-past and we have a deal,' cried Lindy.

Mrs Fraser scowled ferociously. 'There's no need to be cheeky, lassie. You'd need to squeal too, if you were deaf.' Then she waddled off, leaving Lindy to work that out.

At that point Pa's first patient came out, to be replaced by old Mrs Beckett. She really preferred to be seen at home — unless there was a coffee morning or some other such entertainment going on in the town. Lindy was wondering what had brought her out today when the phone rang. She picked it up and listened.

'Right, Mrs Chisholm. Dr Dunbar will be with you as soon as possible.' Another patient to be added to Pa's list, which was already quite long. He's going to be tired tonight, she worried. Thank goodness Lyall only allows him to do one surgery a day. . .

That morning she took the doctors almond biscuits

with their coffee. 'What have I done to deserve this?' wondred Lyall after the first appreciative taste.

'Nothing. I baked more than I need for tonight, that's all.'

'Yes — about tonight. Would you rather call it off after our midnight adventure? You must be worn out.'

'We all have to eat, and I'm well ahead with my preparations,' she returned matter-of-factly. 'Besides, we do want your sister to know she's welcome.'

'As long as you're sure. I know Debbie will appreciate it. What a good little soul you are, he added abruptly.

'Aw, shucks, you're making me blush,' said Lindy, backing out and closing the door. She supposed it was better to be a good little soul than the teenage incompetent he'd thought her at first, but after last night's closeness she'd been hoping he'd manage to see her as a woman. What a tantalising puzzle that man was!

Lindy didn't get the chance of a coffee herself, because by then Mrs Fraser was back. She showed her into the dressing-room. 'I could have had my treatment in here earlier,' decided the patient disgustedly.

'No — this is kept for dressings and splints.' Lindy hadn't spoken loudly enough, and Mrs Fraser put a hand behind her ear. 'Splints, Mrs Fraser — splints!' bawled Lindy.

'Are ye mad? I'm not trying the splits at my age, you cheeky besom! Anyway, how would that help ma hand?'

Muffled sounds of laughter came from both consulting-rooms.

At lunchtime, Lindy decided to tackle her father about Mrs Fraser's increasing deafness. 'Is there nothing to be done, Pa? It must be terribly difficult for her family — never mind my vocal cords.'

'Ellen referred her to an ENT specialist last year, but hers is not the kind of hearing loss that can be helped by an aid.' He frowned at his cottage cheese salad. 'Is this all we're having today?'

'Don't forget dinner will be extra special tonight in Debbie Balfour's honour. What do you recommend for my sore throat, Pa?'

'Try a spoonful of honey,' suggested her father with a chuckle.

'So you think I need sweetening, huh?'

'Any sweeter and you'd be too good for this wicked world, my precious child,' said her father with an unexpected burst of sentiment that rather embarrassed them both.

Lindy took out her hankie and blew her nose rather noisily. 'You silly old fool,' she said gruffly. 'Here, have a scone with your cuppa.'

Fiona was very disappointed that Dr Balfour wasn't there to drive her home that afternoon. Not that she said so, but the way she kept looking out of the window during her treatment and then hung around afterwards was enough. Lindy smiled to herself as she rolled up her white coat and stuffed it into a plastic carrier bag. 'Give me your bag and I'll strap it to my bike, Fiona,' she said. 'I'm starting on your wee brother today.'

'You'll not find him as patient as I am,' warned the child, as Lindy hoisted her on to the saddle, and replied, 'The weans never are as patient as big girls like you.' But Fiona was only big in heart. Her thin little face and stick-like legs were proof of that. All the same, the child was pleased with the compliment, and that was what mattered.

Lindy's heart sank when she was ushered into the Duffus living-room and saw Calum for the first time. Vividly she recalled Fiona saying that her granny didn't think he'd make old bones. She strove to be positive in the face of his mother's anxiety. 'You've not been back in Eyretoun very long, Mrs Duffus. He'll soon pick up in our good country air. Look how well Fiona's doing.' Lindy sat down and took Calum on her knee. 'I hope you like fudge, young man, 'cos I've brought you some I made myself. But not till we've had a go at this wee chest of yours.' She tickled his ribs, making him chortle.

'I'm away to do ma homework, Mammy,' said Fiona, who couldn't bear to watch her brother having his physio.

Cycling home afterwards, Lindy worried all the way. Was it wrong to raise Mrs Duffus's spirits when Calum was obviously worse than Fiona? Yet agreeing with her fears would only make things worse, would it not? I must ask Ellen what line to take. I should have asked her before I went. Oh, why do I never seem to get anything right? And she didn't just mean professionally. Already she was blaming herself for Lyall's drawing back the night before. Was it possible she had pushed too hard? But heavens, look at the time! She wouldn't manage to squeeze in that reviving bath she'd been promising herself all day if she didn't speed up.

But somehow it all got done. The soup was ready for last-minute heating, the casserole was smelling delicious as it bubbled gently the oven, the lemon mousse had moussed properly instead of separating, and, just when she'd given up hope, the grocer's boy arrived with the cheeses. A last glance at the dining table to make sure she'd forgotten nothing and Lindy could dash upstairs for that longed-for soak.

In her mind she had formed a picture of Debbie Balfour. She would be tall and elegant and as cool and sophisticated as her brother. So the last thing Lindy expected was the small, plumpish, merry-eyed brunette who burst into the sitting-room, overflowing with goodwill and *joie de vivre*. She took to her on sight. So too did her father and Ellen, judging by the warmth of their welcome. Lyall stood aside, watching complacently as his sister made herself at home in the space of minutes.

As soon as they all had drinks, Lindy's father proposed a toast. 'To our new practice nurse. May she be as happy in her work here as the rest of us.'

They all drank to that — Debbie as well — before she said, 'And now I've got something I simply must get off my chest. I think it's fantastic the way you, Dr Dunbar and you, Dr Frew, agreed to take me on unseen. So I'm insisting on a month's trial. I'll know by then whether I fit in or not and, if I don't, then I shall take myself off the payroll. And that's a promise.'

As Ellen said, nobody could say fairer than that, and it was a very harmonious little party that presently sat down to enjoy Lindy's dinner. It went like a celebration, thanks to Debbie's eagerness to please and be pleased, and afterwards she insisted on being the one to help Lindy clear the table. 'Besides, I want to talk to you,' she added, padding after Lindy to the kitchen.

First, though, she helped herself to the last of the almond biscuits that had accompanied the mousse. 'Sorry to be such a pig — I just couldn't resist it. Lyall's right — you are the most marvellous cook.'

But what does he really think of me in other respects? wondered Lindy, as she spooned coffee into the biggest cafetière.

As if she were a mind-reader, Debbie said, 'He also told me you've been running the surgeries all by yourself since the last nurse left.'

'Not all of them — there's a super retired sister who does three evenings a week for us. And she's much better at it than I.'

'That's not what Lyall says,' his sister denied

promptly. 'But he does think it's rather a waste of a good physio.'

'Not really — I'd have been out of a job otherwise.'

'He told me that too.' Debbie watched Lindy piling fudge into a small glass dish. 'Don't tell me you made that! Is there anything you can't do?'

Make your brother fall in love with me! Lindy blushed at a thought she didn't even know had been lurking there in her subconscious. 'I gave up my job to come home and look after Pa when he had his coronary,' she threw in quickly. 'Any daughter would have done the same.'

'I can think of several who wouldn't have,' retorted Debbie. 'I mean, you couldn't have had any idea they were going to be able to wangle you a post in the practice, could you?'

'That was the last thing I expected.'

'Well, I'm jolly glad, I can tell you. I'd have felt awful, taking over and leaving you high and dry — in fact, I think I'd have refused. I've been wanting to tell you that.'

'But we're each to get the job we can do best,' said Lindy. 'And now I'd better make this coffee. The kettle boiled ages ago.'

'We were having a lovely gossip,' she explained comfortably when her father said he thought they'd run away.

'I hope we've not made a mistake, partners,' said Lyall. 'I mean, if these two are going to natter away all day, instead of getting on with the work. . .' He had to duck to avoid his sister's clenched fist.

'Of course you three never spoke a word while we were slaving away in the kitchen,' Lindy supported her.

'Well done, that girl!' cried Debbie. 'I couldn't have put things better myself.'

'One thing's for sure, life'll not be dull with you two around,' said Ellen, helping herself to a handful of fudge. 'But I hope you'll not be as late with the morning coffee as you were with this — I've got to dash now. I'm the unlucky so-and-so who's on call tonight, and I've a couple of patients I want to look in on on my way home.' She shook hands with Debbie, who was now looking faintly worried. 'Glad you've come, lassie. If you work half as hard as your brother, you'll do.'

'Do you think Dr Frew was really cross?' asked Debbie anxiously when Ellen had gone.

'Not at all,' denied Dr Dunbar. 'She never drinks coffee at night — says it keeps her awake. But she does like her little joke. You'll get used to it, my dear.'

The party broke up soon after that. Debbie was tired after her long drive and the others were all feeling the effects of last night's emergency. As they said goodnight, Lindy told Debbie she'd be along to lend a hand the next afternoon.

'I knew I was going to like you the minute I saw you,' said Debbie by way of thanks before a chorus of goodnights all round.

'What a delightful girl,' approved Dr Dunbar as he locked the front door. 'She will be a much nicer friend for you than Elspeth.'

He's psychic, thought Lindy. She'd been thinking the same thing herself.

Mrs Turnbull wasn't due for treatment the next day, but she looked in all the same, breathless with the news of an enormous pantechnicon outside the Bank. 'I heard the new doctor had taken the flat over it, so that'll be him moving in,' she assumed. 'But who's the strange young woman directing operations, I'd like to know? We all ken he's not married, so what'll folk be making of that?' she wound up, all but smacking her lips.

'Not a lot,' returned Lindy, positively bursting for once to satisfy her curiosity. 'It would be Dr Balfour's sister you saw. She arrived yesterday.'

Naturally Mrs Turnbull found that very disappointing, having thought herself on the track of a nice juicy scandal. As soon as Lindy had seen her off the premises, she filled her basket with a selection from her stores and set off for the flat in the High Street.

The removal men were only just driving off and Debbie was hanging out of a window waving goodbye. When she saw Lindy she called out, 'Hello there! Come right on up — the door is open.'

Lindy remembered the layout from the days when the manager was still expected to live on the spot, and she went straight into the drawing-room, where Debbie was raking through a trunk. 'Isn't this chaotic?' she asked cheerfully. 'I'd expected to be further on than this by now, but the men were two hours late and then they had a devil of a job getting the piano up the stairs.'

A handsome Steinway grand, it dominated the room. 'I'm not surprised,' said Lindy.

'I'd have left it in store with the bulk of our stuff until we found a house, but Lyall couldn't bear to be parted from it any longer, even though he can't play it much these days.'

Because of the accident, Lindy thought sympathetically as Debbie hurried on, 'I'm trying to find some bedlinen. If I can get our bedrooms done and clear a space to sit, then that will do for today. Ah, here we are,' she cried in triumph. 'Great! Now how about a cup of tea?'

'Why do we not make the beds first?' Lindy asked

practically. 'It's much easier with two. And I did come to help, remember.'

'You're so sensible!' exclaimed Debbie admiringly, seizing an armful of bedding and tossing it over. 'Right! Follow me.'

All her brother's energy but without the reserve, decided Lindy, following Debbie up the second flight of stairs. 'I got the curtains hung while the men were bringing in the furniture,' Debbie rattled on. 'Lord, what a job! Twice I nearly fell off the steps. They don't quite fit, but they'll keep us decent, and there's no point in buying new when we're only here temporarily.'

With the bedrooms more or less habitable, they went down to the kitchen. 'Now for that tea,' said Debbie, raking around for the kettle. 'Sorry about the biscuits, but there wasn't much selection in the shop next door. Is there another grocer?'

'We've always gone to the one next door to the chemist's further up the road. I've brought you a few things,' Lindy added modestly, hoisting her basket on to the table.

Debbie fell on it eagerly. 'Oh, Lindy, what a pal you are! Shortbread — my favourite! This is going to be a feast. Let's have it in the sitting-room.'

She had already arranged chairs around the empty fireplace, so they were able to relax in comfort. Debbie looked at the walls. 'I'd have this room a lot lighter if we were staying but we hope to be out before the winter.'

'You've got somthing in mind,' assumed Lindy.

'Not yet, but we're optimists. Well, I am anyway.' Debbie's expression grew dreamy. 'What we'd both absolutely love is to get the old manse, but unfortunately it's not on the market. Did you know our father was born in that house?'

'No, but I did know about your grandfather being minister at the West Kirk.'

'When he realised he'd have to change direction, Lyall became obsessed with the idea of coming to Scotland, but he never dreamed he'd have the luck to get into practice right here in Eyretoun.'

'Giving up surgery must have been a great blow,' said Lindy, relying on Debbie's spontaneity for further enlightenment.

She wasn't entirely disappointed. 'So simply done, yet so terrible in consequence. Who'd have thought a glass door would shatter like that? Still, with that bitch in one of her tempers——' Debbie stopped short. 'Anyway, the flexor tendons were ripped to ribbons, so it's a miracle the hand functions as well as it does. His fine movments are impaired, though really you'd hardly notice—and occasionally he gets the most awful cramp. Poor Lyall! He had a hell of a time coming to terms with the collapse of his life's ambition. Let me top you up, Lindy.'

'Thanks.' Lindy passed her cup, saying sincerely, 'He's adapted remarkably well. My father is delighted with him.

'Is he really? I'm so glad—Lyall has such respect for him.'

That was really good to know. 'And now of course your brother wants to forget his disappointment and concentrate on the present,' Lindy summed up.

'Absolutely! A completely new start, with all aspects of his unhappy past behind him.'

Good grief! Was there some other horror as well? Something to do with 'that bitch' Debbie had referred to, perhaps? No wonder he often looked so gloomy! But Lindy got no chance to think more about that, because Debbie was saying with unusual awkwardness, 'And talking of unhappy pasts, I guess Lyall has told you I'm divorced.'

'He did mention it — and now we're all hoping that returning to a place of which you have such happy memories — making new friends and keeping busy — will help you to get yourself together again.'

'Thanks, Lindy! What a capacity you have for saying the right thing,' said Debbie gratefully.

It'd be nice to think your brother agreed with you, Lindy was musing when the downstairs door slammed, somebody took the stairs two at a time and the man himself came in. His eyes went straight to Lindy, workmanlike in jeans and a much-washed old shirt. 'So you did come,' he said warmly. 'I was sure you would, and it's very kind of you.'

'And we've been so busy,' Debbie told him.

'So I see,' said her brother, casting a superior smile in the direction of the teacups.

'Don't bother thinking up any wisecracks,' ordered Debbie. 'We've only just sat down.'

'The tea will still be fresh, then. I'll fetch myself a cup.'

'And bring the kettle for a top-up,' Debbie instructed. She turned back to Lindy. 'I thought we might try and straighten out the kitchen next — if you've got time.'

'I can stay as long as you need me, Debbie. My father's been asked out for his supper tonight.'

'That's all right, then.'

'What is?' asked Lyall, returning just then.

'Lindy's going to help me with the kitchen while you put up those curtains in here.' Debbie pointed to a pile of soft green velvet on the windowseat.

Lyall sat down and grinned crookedly at Lindy. 'And you think I'm a slavedriver!'

'That's obviously a family trait,' she ventured, smiling

back. How much easier it was for them to talk in
Debbie's lively presence.

He told her she didn't know the half of it, while
Debbie wondered how he dared say such a thing when
everybody knew she was the mildest creature in the
world.

During that exchange, Lindy was struggling to keep
her eyes from straying to Lyall's right hand. Could he
cope with the job his sister had earmarked for him?

'I say, this is superb!' exclaimed Lyall after biting into
a piece of shortbread. 'No prizes for guessing who made
it.'

'At least you've never found fault with my baking,'
Lindy said provocatively.

'Nobody ever finds fault with perfection if they're
wise,' he declared.

'Very true,' said Debbie. 'But just in case you're
thinking of making a pig of yourself with another bit,
kindly remember the curtains.' Then she bent over him
to say in a low voice, 'That's if you think you can
manage, duckie.'

He threw a playful punch in her direction. 'I'll manage
if it kills me. So off to the kitchen with you, you cheeky
besom. That's much the best place for you.'

It really was astonishing how much more relaxed he
was now Debbie had come. And not the least bit snooty
now, either. In this mood, it was easy to see why
everybody liked him. Which posed a question for Lindy.
Why was it only with her that he seemed so constrained?

Two hours later, the kitchen was knee-deep in dis-
carded wrapping paper, but all the crates had been
unpacked and their contents stashed away in cupboards.
When Lyall came through to say he had run out of
things to do, Lindy was on her hands and knees, cleaning
the oven. 'What on earth. . .?' he began. 'Debs, you

really are the limit! Lindy shouldn't be doing that!' He
sounded quite angry.

'I only turned my back for a minute and she'd started.
Short of heaving her bodily out of the way, how could I
have stopped her?'

'I've nearly finished,' Lindy reported, looking up for a
minute and pushing her shoulder-length hair out of her
eyes. That left a dirty streak on her forehead. She
plunged into action again.

'Finished or not, you're stopping right now — and then
we're all going out for a meal,' said Lyall, swooping
down and hoisting Lindy up and clean off her feet. 'Who
the hell can that be?' he wondered, forgetting to put her
down when the doorbell rang. She was dangling there
under his arm like a bundle of washing.

'I'll go,' volunteered Debbie, dashing out.

'Do you not think you should put me down before you
do your back in?' Lindy asked breathlessly. She was
surprised she had managed to speak at all. This sudden
close contact with Lyall was having all sorts of unsettling
effects.

'If I did, I'm sure you'd soon fix it,' he returned.
Having set her down, he eyed her thoughtfully before
saying, 'D'you realise those damn curtains are heavier
than you?'

'Good things come in small parcels,' she was telling
him when Debbie returned with Elspeth.

'A friend of yours, I understand, Lyall,' said his sister
in a neutral voice.

Elspeth looked immaculate as usual in yet another
new outfit. Her golden hair had obviously been re-gilded
that very afternoon. She set a formal floral arrangement
on the table, taking care not to damage her long tapering
red nails. 'Just a little offering for your new home——'
She broke off when she realised who it was hiding behind

Lyall. 'Lindy! Heavens, what a sight you are! Your face is filthy. What *have* you been doing?'

'Helping us,' Debbie told her crisply, just as Lyall said, 'I don't imagine you've ever cleaned an oven, Elspeth, but it's not the cleanest of jobs.'

Lindy just stood there feeling hurt. Elspeth was supposed to be her friend.

Elspeth's confident smile faltered ever so slightly. 'If I'd realised you were needing help, I'd have come sooner. But if there's anything left to do. . .'

Somebody put as much as a duster in her hand and she'll faint, guessed Lindy. Both Balfours rejected her offer, as they were meant to.

'About food, then,' said Elspeth. 'You'll not be wanting to cook tonight, but if you'd care to come round to my place, I could rustle up something acceptable . . .' She looked from brother to sister and back again, just managing not to include Lindy in the invitation.

Debbie at least noticed. 'It's very kind of you, but Lindy has already provided us with a basketful of goodies,' she said firmly. 'Another time, perhaps.'

'That's a date,' said Elspeth, not too pleased at finding herself outwitted. She gave Lindy a spiteful look and said she might as well be going if her help wasn't wanted.

'I'll see you out,' said Lyall.

As they left the room, Lindy waved a grimy hand towards her basket. 'Only an apple pie and some cakes and things, so perhaps you should have accepted ——'

'I know what you've brought us, because I've already looked,' said Debbie. 'But I didn't take to that lady, and if I'd told her that Lyall had already decided to take us out for supper she'd very likely have tagged along.' She frowned worriedly. 'I don't understand what he's about there. I'd have thought he'd had enough of her sort.'

Her sort? What *did* Debbie mean? But here was Lyall back already. Elspeth must be slipping.

He smiled crookedly at his sister and ruffled her hair affectionately. 'I can read you like a book,' he claimed. 'You didn't take to Elspeth, did you? So I resisted the temptation to ask her to join us.'

'Ten out of ten for intuition,' said Debbie.

'And I really ought to be getting along,' said Lindy, just in case he'd felt obliged to include her and didn't really want to. Just as always, Elspeth had left her feeling inadequate.

'Nonsense!' Lyall said positively. 'The least we can do is feed you when you've done so much for us.'

Lindy was also bothered about her shabby old clothes. 'But I look such a mess! The best thing I could do would be to sneak off home by the back road.'

'You look no worse than we do,' insisted Lyall, showing off the crumpled trousers and baggy old sweater into which he'd changed before tackling the curtains. 'No changing, Debs, you hear? Just a quick wash all round and then we'll sample the food at a nice little inn I noticed the other day out on the Kelso road. Lindy, you shall have the bathroom first.'

So he really meant for her to join them, and with Pa eating out tonight Lindy hadn't been looking forward to a solitary supper. Twenty minutes later they were all in Lyall's car and heading out of town.

The road to the inn lay past the Robertsons' farm-house. It was a sizeable, handsome Georgian place, surrounded by lush parkland dotted with majestic old trees. The farm buildings were some distance from the house and completely screened by a small grove of conifers.

'Now that's exactly the sort of house I'd like,'

announced Debbie, craning round for another look as they passed.

'We'd better introduce her to Andy, then,' said Lyall with a broad wink for Lindy. 'The farmer's son,' he explained over his shoulder. 'Of course, his affections are more or less engaged elsewhere, but that's a minor detail.'

'Talking of whom——' said Lindy, waving to a lone horseman trotting towards them.

Lyall slowed the car and Andy reined in. His face showed a disappointment which gave way to pleasure when he realised it wasn't Elspeth, but Lindy sitting beside the driver. 'I'd like you to meet my sister,' said Lyall. 'She's just fallen in love with your house.'

'Then she's got taste,' said Andy, dismounting to view Debbie's dark prettiness with approval.

Debbie, though rather embarrased, made the best of it. 'I'm also very taken with your horse, Mr Robertson,' she said when Lyall had made the introductions.

'Andy, please. Do you ride yourself, then?'

'Sadly not for some time now, but I used to.'

'If you ever feel like taking it up again, just you get in touch. We can always find you a suitable mount.'

'I'd like that very much.'

'Good,' said Andy, his approval increasing.

Lindy was worried. She was afraid he might be seeing Debbie as a way of getting even with Elspeth, and she reckoned that Debbie had had enough trouble lately, without being used as a pawn in somebody else's games.

'I suppose you've all been for a walk,' said Andy.

'No—moving house,' they chorused. 'And now we're off to get something to eat at that place,' added Lyall, pointing towards the inn.

'Then I shall stable Border Lad and join you,' decided

Andy. 'I've already eaten, but a pint of heavy never comes amiss.'

The evening was warm, so they chose an outside table, and were halfway through their meal when Andy came. He was still in riding kit, which suited his athletic build. In spite of having broken his nose on the rugby field, he was really very nice-looking, Lindy realised. And she'd certainly never known him quite so chatty. Debbie was fairly drawing him out.

The shadows lengthened and the sun was setting, so they transferred to the bar. But the talk was flowing as freely as ever, and eventually the landlord had to beg them to go home before he lost his licence.

'We must do this again — and soon,' said Andy decisively when they left him at the gates to the farm.

'What a nice man,' said Debbie as they drove on.

'And I think you've made a conquest, our Debs,' teased her brother, smiling.

'But you told me his affections were already engaged,' she reminded him. 'All the same, I hope he remembers offering to lend me a horse. Those there hills were just made for trekking over.'

When they got to Downside House, Lyall got out of the car and walked up the drive with Lindy. 'I don't know how to begin to thank you for helping Debbie the way you did,' he said warmly.

'Oh, I like being useful — even if it's only a little bit.'

'What nonsense!' he insisted.

'Are you saying you don't believe I like to be useful?' Lindy challenged.

'Of course you enjoy being useful — it was one of the first things I noticed about you. It's the "little bit" I'm refuting. You've been the greatest help — and I can't believe you don't know it.' The words were reproving, but his tone was very gentle.

'You're telling me off again,' said Lindy in a small voice. 'I can see I've still got to be very careful what I say to you.'

'But not too careful, I hope,' he drawled softly. 'Who's to keep me in line if you don't?'

'Is that how it seemed?'

'That's how it was.'

'You're too clever by half,' she murmured.

'And you are — very refreshing.'

'So is a nice long drink of Perrier water. Are you not afraid I might get above myself if you pay me compliments like that?'

'If you do, I shall know exactly how to deal with you,' he promised on a chuckle. 'I shall simply give you a dose of the disapproval you meted out to me when first I came.'

'Oh dear!' she breathed with exaggerated pathos.

'So now you know what to expect,' he threatened, leaning down and kissing her softly parted lips.

Lindy was enchanted for the three seconds it took him to decide that had been another mistake. Then he brushed her playfully under the chin with the back of his hand. 'What a beguiling little minx you are, Lindsay Dunbar,' he breathed on a throaty chuckle before saying a careless 'Goodnight' and striding away down the drive.

CHAPTER SIX

SATURDAY morning surgeries were rarely busy, and Lindy could never decide whether that was because the patients wanted their Saturdays for leisure, or because they thought that the doctors did. This one was no exception, with only six patients booked in so far.

Except for brief professional exchanges in the surgery, Lindy had seen little of Lyall since the second brush-off, on the doorstep, last Wednesday night. I wonder how long he thinks it'll take me to get the message, she wondered, as she looked out the records for Surgery. A week? Two weeks? At least that. Don't forget he thinks you're thick, even though these days he tries to hide it, so he'll not be taking any chances.

'You look like you've lost a fiver and found one of those daft wee five-pence pieces,' reckoned Ellen, coming in just then and recalling Lindy to the present.

'Do I? Then could be I'm pining,' she answered with a big smile to show she didn't really mean that. 'This is my last week but one as surgery dogsbody, remember.'

'So it is,' remembered Ellen. 'What will you do with yourself until your new treatment-room is ready?'

'I'm going to Switzerland to stay with a friend I trained with. She's got a wonderful job out there in a private clinic. We fixed it up by phone last night,' Lindy added, trying to look overjoyed at the idea and not sure she was succeeding.

'That's splendid, lassie,' approved Ellen. 'You're quite right to go while you've got the chance.' She was a great believer in holidays for everybody except herself. 'So how many have you got lined up for me today?'

Lindy handed her the records. 'And here's your first patient now,' she said as Miss Simpson, all stout and harassed, puffed into the waiting-room.

She waddled obediently after Ellen as two more patients drifted in. Both had appointments. Lindy ticked them off and wondered whether it was too soon to start tidying some cupboards. She meant to leave everything in perfect order for Debbie's takeover, but do it too soon and the doctors would only mess everything up again.

Miss Simpson reappeared. 'Dr Frew's wantin' me to have a splint for my wrist, dear. Seems I've got some sort of -itis in it.'

Lindy looked at the note Ellen had sent. 'Tenosynovitis is inflammation of the sheaths that protect the muscle tendons from wear and tear as they glide over the bones of the wrist joint, Miss Simpson. I'm afraid it's usually rather painful.'

'Agony, more like. You'd never believe it! And Father never satisfied. "Do this, Nan. Do that, Nan. Whaur's ma tea, Nan. . .?"'

'He'll have to look after himself when you're in the hospital, though.' Miss Simpson was on the waiting list for an operation on her varicose veins.

'Aye, so he will, the auld divil. Mebbe he'll appreciate me a bit more after that. Ouch!'

'Sorry about that,' apologised Lindy, 'but once I get this fixed you'll be much more comfortable. You will keep it on for as long as Dr Frew said, will you not?'

'Don't you be fretting about that, hen. I'm not thrawn like the auld feller. Do you know. . .?' She was away again, and during that recital of her father's shortcomings Lyall came into the dressing-room. He hovered for a bit, but after a casual nod Lindy ignored him. He was off duty, so he couldn't be needing her help. So she left him there, opening and shutting cupboards, while she escorted Miss Simpson out. Good thing I didn't start on my tidying, she was thinking.

When she went back, Lyall was still there. 'I'm sorry to bother you,' he said politely, 'but I can't find any six-inch crêpe bandages.'

'We don't keep any. Space is so limited, and there's not much call for them.'

'But this morning I visited a patient whose stump bandages have about as much give in them as a piece of string.'

'Joe Burnett,' she guessed.

He stared. 'How on earth did you know that?'

'From your description. There isn't any other patient it could be. If you care to write out a prescription, I'll call at the chemist's and deliver them this afternoon.'

'I couldn't possibly put you to that trouble, Lindy,' he protested.

'It's no trouble. I have to shop this afternoon and I'll pass his house later on my way to the Duffuses'.'

His eyebrows rose. 'Does that mean you treat those children every day?'

'Not quite. I don't on Sundays.'

'That's — very, very good of you,' he told her with apparent sincerity.

Lindy shrugged. 'Most folk have their better moments — even me! But you'll have to excuse me. Ellen is calling for me.' She wasn't too pleased with that. It didn't fit in with the cool detachment she'd been trying to project. How to do better next time?

But when Lindy returned after finding Ellen's auro-scope under a pile of papers, Lyall had gone into the other consulting-room. He didn't come out again until surgery was over and Lindy was making coffee. 'That smells good,' he said.

'Does that mean you'd like some?' she asked casually without turning round. That was better!

'Am I entitled?' he asked with a forced little laugh. 'After all, I'm not on duty.'

'I imagine that means yes,' she returned, spooning more coffee into the cafetière. 'I'll bring this to your room when it's brewed.'

'Is there any rule which says I can't have it here?'

'None that I know of.' Neither was there a rule which said he couldn't invite her into his consulting-room to be talked to—but then he was probably afraid she might shut the door and Ellen might get ideas! 'I take it then that there's a problem?'

He raised an eyebrow. 'No—no problem, but it is time we started thinking about equipment for your new room.'

'I've already made out a list, on the basis of patients seen so far and those most likely to be referred in the future.'

'That's very far-sighted of you, but as we want everything to be as up to date as possible I'd like you to take a run up to Edinburgh to talk to staff at the Southern General Hospital. I'm told theirs is the most up-to-date department in the city.'

'Will it do when I come back from holiday?' asked Lindy. 'It takes all day by bus, and I don't see how I can get away while I still have the surgeries to see to.'

'The room will be almost ready by then, so I'd rather not leave it that long. But if you could get one of your helpers to take evening surgery on Wednesday next you could come with me. I have to go to Edinburgh in the afternoon to talk finance.'

'I'm sure somebody will swap if it's really that urgent,'

Lindy returned evenly. 'But now I'd better speed up,' she added in response to a loud call from Ellen. 'She doesn't function too well without her elevenses.'

'Debbie was wondering if you and your father would like to join us for supper tonight,' Lyall said quickly.

'How very kind of her — I'll give her a ring shortly. I'm sure my father would be delighted, but I'm going to a barn dance with Bill.'

'I'm sure that will be much more to your taste,' Lyall said quietly.

'Because I'm a bit of a hayseed,' Lindy agreed as Ellen gave vent to another bellow. 'Coming!' she yelled back, cutting across Lyall's exclamation of protest. When she returned to the tiny kitchen, he had gone.

Wednesday morning was dragging. Not that Lindy was short of things to do; when was she ever during a surgery? But dragging it was. Strange, that.

As soon as she'd made lists of the house calls and looked out the morning's records, she had rung her own patients to remind them that their afternoon appointments were cancelled. Except of course for the Duffus children, whom she'd be visiting at home that evening.

Mrs Turnbull repeated the fuss she'd made on Monday. 'I really do not know what the NHS is coming to,' she grumbled.

Lindy wanted to ask what the NHS had to do with it, when she was currently working for nothing. Instead she retorted, 'I'm not going to Edinburgh for fun, you know. This is a business trip.'

'Talking of which, I thought that Debbie Balfour was supposed to be here on business, so what was she doing out riding last night with Andy Robertson? Tell me that!'

Lindy mentally filed away that interesting snippet for

consideration later and offered to fit Mrs Turnbull in the following afternoon.

'What! On early closing day when I always go to see my friend in Melrose? I never heard the like! I can see I'll just have to thole it till Friday. Is there anything going on there?'

Lindy knew quite well that Mrs Turnbull was curious about Andy and Debbie, but she pretended to misunderstand. 'In Melrose? I think there is — the Annual Rose Show. See you on Friday, then, Mrs Turnbull.' She put down the phone on the postmistress's frustrated splutterings.

So Andy and Debbie had gone riding together already — and now she knew why he hadn't shown up at the Eyretoun Arms the night before. Lindy wondered if Elspeth had known; she'd certainly been in a filthy mood, and had needed little excuse to take herself off. Not that the evening had improved. Lindy had been unable to keep her mind off today's Edinburgh jaunt, and Bill had also seemed preoccupied. She'd never got home from such a meeting so early before.

She was jerked out of her musings by Ellen calling out plaintively to know how much longer she'd got to wait for her coffee. 'Just coming!' Lindy yelled back with more optimism than accuracy, considering she hadn't even got the kettle on.

'It's a damn good thing I've not got many visits today,' grumbled Ellen when Lindy eventually steamed into her room, slopping coffee into the saucer in her haste. She mopped up with a tissue and told Ellen she was getting right crabbit in her old age, before taking coffee to Lyall.

For once he wasn't dictating, but lounging back in his chair and gazing moodily into space. Something's upset him, she realised. She wanted to ask what, but that wouldn't have fitted in with her present attitude of casual detachment. An English newspaper was spread carelessly on the desk, but it couldn't be anything he'd just read that was responsible; the paper was open at the fashion page, quite half of which was taken up by a photograph of a beautiful blonde, pouting disdainfully out of a great swath of tulle.

'You are needing your elevenses,' Lindy decided firmly.

Lyall came to with a start. 'How did you guess?' he asked with determined lightness.

'Because you were looking very jaded, and I'm a good ten minutes late with it this morning.'

'Brilliant reasoning.' With sudden decision, he crumpled up the paper and stuffed it in the wastepaper basket. 'As a matter of fact, I was wondering how best to put our case for extra funding when I talk to the all-powerful ones this afternoon,' he said, just as though she'd asked for an explanation.

Pull the other one, she thought, while pretending to believe him. 'You'll certainly need all your wits and powers of persuasion,' she agreed.

He gave a careful smile. 'Do you think I'll be equal to the challenge?'

'I don't doubt that for a moment. Anybody who can galvanise the local tradesmen into action the way you have is more than a match for a few civil servants.'

'Your confidence in me is most — encouraging.'

Lindy met his glance unblinking. 'The last thing you're short of is confidence, Dr Lyall Balfour. I never met any man better at getting folk to dance to his tune.'

'I'd give a lot to know exactly what you meant by that,' he said thoughtfully.

'*I'm* not devious,' she returned pointedly. 'So you may take it I meant exactly what I said.'

'Are you suggesting that I am?'

'That you are what?'

'Devious.'

Oh, goody, you got the point! she thought. 'Enigmatic is probably a better word. I simply do not know what to make of you, and that's a fact.'

'I don't blame you,' he said with sudden heat. 'Most of the time, I don't know what the hell to make of myself!'

Now there was a surprise. And how well timed was Ellen's bellow for help from the next room, because Lindy hadn't a clue how to answer him. 'I'm neglecting my duties,' she observed needlessly before going to Ellen's rescue.

At last the morning was over—lunch too—and Lindy could go upstairs to get ready. After a lot of mind-changing, she eventually settled on a dark flowered skirt with matching blouse worn open over a toning designer T-shirt. A necklace of coral and some high-heeled sandals added the touch of formality needed for a trip to that most conservative of cities. After all, she didn't want her ex-colleagues thinking she'd gone to seed down here in the backwoods. For the same reason, she made up her face much more carefully than usual, feeling quite pleased with the result. At the last minute, she remembered why she was going and popped a notebook in her bag.

Lyall was punctual as usual; Ellen was right when she said you could set the clock by him. He looked cool and collected in perfectly tailored trousers worn with an open-necked shirt and a quiet silk cravat. A light jacket hung from a hook inside the car. He eyed Lindy with sober approval before saying, 'You're looking very charming and grown-up.'

So they were back to that, were they? 'I can't halt the

passage of time any more than anybody else,' she
retorted crisply. He smiled at that. But if he dares to
ruffle my hair or—or pat me on the back, she thought,
I'll. . .!

He didn't. He opened the car door for her, then bent
down to tuck in her skirt when it flowed out over the sill.
That brought his face very close to hers. The faint
muskiness of his after-shave evoked a funny little *fris-
son*—plus a rather worried frown. Doubtfuully she
watched him walk round to the driver's side. I've got to
be very careful, she told herself. He may say he doesn't
know his own mind, and maybe in some areas that's
true, but he's made it very plain that he knows his own
mind where I'm concerned. So the sooner I stop moon-
ing over him, the better!

Lyall didn't set off directly as she'd expected, and she
could feel him looking at her again. 'Have I got a smut
on my nose?' she demanded haughtily.

'No—just a light dusting of freckles.'

'Which I can't do anything about.'

'Why would you want to? They suit you.'

Never mind the buttering up—we both know it
doesn't mean a thing! 'I'll bet,' Lindy almost snarled.
'Little schoolgirl image, and all that.'

He shrugged. 'If you say so. Most women are glad to
know they look younger than they are.'

'Not at my age, they're not. Of course, if it's still true
when I'm fifty, I expect I'll be glad.'

His continued scrutiny was so thorough that Lindy
was hard put to it not to blush. 'Your bone structure is
good, so it probably will be,' he decided.

To be complimented on your bone structure when
beauty was said to be only skin deep was not exactly
exhilarating. Lindy decided a complete change of subject

was called for. 'I can hardly believe I've only three more days to go as practice nurse,' she observed chattily.

'Ouch!' exclaimed Lyall unexpectedly as he set the car going at last.

Lindy glanced at him in surprise but said nothing, not having grasped the point he was making. 'You think that was all pre-planned, don't you?' he challenged.

'You mean—Debbie getting the job? Whether it was or not, it's certainly worked out very conveniently.'

'An instance of getting folk to dance to my tune, perhaps?'

'Perhaps, perhaps not. But I'm not holding *that* against you. I like your sister very much.'

'That's good, because she's taken a great liking to you.' After a few quiet seconds he asked, 'Why did you want to change the subject, Lindy?'

Rapidly she thought back. 'We'd been talking about me—and I decided it was high time we stopped.'

'Really?' Lyall sounded as if he could hardly believe that. 'I thought that was a subject women never tired of.'

'Only the gorgeous ones. Us country mice get too self-conscious.'

He snorted. 'You may be any number of things, but one thing you most definitely are not is a mouse!'

'All right, so what am I, then?' Despite her resolve to be sensible, Lindy was remembering very vividly hearing him call her a beguiling little minx. Would he remember that too?

'I thought you said we'd talked about you long enough,' he answered maddeningly.

There was a lot of traffic on the main road north, and as not enough of it was being driven sensibly, Lyall was having to concentrate hard. He appeared to have forgotten his passenger, but she was acutely aware of him.

Eventually she gave up the struggle to look straight ahead and allowed herself a sideways glance. What a good profile he had; straight nose, strong mouth, determined jaw. . . Add a clear tanned skin, a deep resonant voice, wit, intelligence ——

The corner of Lyall's mouth began to twitch, and Lindy turned away in confusion. But it was his own thoughts that were amusing him. 'I wouldn't mind betting that what really riled you was being mistaken for the maid,' he said.

Quickly she collected her wits. 'Less than being seen as a glaikit schoolgirl.'

'Come again?' he queried.

'Glaikit. Thick, foolish, not the full shilling.'

'Schoolgirl, yes. Stupid, never.' He wasn't going to risk mispronouncing the Scots word.

'That's something, I suppose,' Lindy admitted.

'It's a very great deal.'

'It is? And I'd always thought men preferred silly women.'

'That depends on the context. Brainless females, however gorgeous, have no place in the NHS, for example. They could be lethal.'

'I've known a few men in the NHS who hadn't the nous to run a sweetie shop!' Lindy retorted tartly. How daft of her to imagine, even for a moment, that his going back to talking about her had any personal element in it. All he'd been telling her, really, was that he'd been glad to discover she wasn't totally simple, or he'd never have agreed to her having a permanent job in the practice!

They crested the last rise, and there was Edinburgh spread below and bathed in sunshine. On one side, its serried skyline was silhouetted against the Pentland Hills, and on the other it was divided from the misty contours of Fife by the sparkling silver ribbon of the Forth.

'I'll drop you off at the Southern and pick you up somewhere around three-thirty. All right?' asked Lyall as the colossal outline of the hospital loomed ahead.

Lindy also knew how to be formal—and accomodating. 'Thank you, that should give me ample time. Just drop me at the gate and save yourself some time.'

He glanced down at her sandals. 'I prefer to save you the walk.'

The senior in charge of outpatient physio was an old friend of Lindy's and was delighted to show her round the newly upgraded department, which, as Lyall had discovered, had the very latest in electrotherapy equipment. An hour flew past in discussion, by which time Lindy had made a list of the units which would best meet the requirements of patients in an outpatient clinic.

'All the same, I'd really like one of the new electronic joint exercisers, Jeannie,' she said wistfully. 'It'd save me such a lot of verbal effort.'

'It's an awful lot of money for something that would be lying idle for much of the time,' argued her friend. 'Now if I were you, I'd go for another——' She stopped abruptly, her eyes wide. 'I say! Look at that gorgeous man who's just come in. I hope he's on my list.'

Lindy turned round and saw Lyall. 'Sorry to disappoint a pal,' she laughed, 'but that's my father's new partner, come to pick me up.'

'And to think we were all so sorry for you, marooned down there among the hills and the sheep!'

Lindy just had time to tell Jeannie that as far as he was concerned, his partner's daughter was nothing but a useful pair of hands, before Lyall came up to them. Introductions were made, Lyall thanked Jeannie warmly for all her help and she offered them tea. 'How very kind of you,' he said, 'but we really don't have time.'

'Are you on evening surgery, then?' asked Lindy as they set off down endless corridors, to the car park.

'No, this is my half-day.'

'Then why the hurry—not that it's any of my business?' she added hurriedly.

'It is—in a way,' he said haltingly. 'I was thinking of taking the long way home, round by St Mary's Loch. But of course if you're in a hurry——'

'But I'm not!' How gormless of her to sound so eager! 'As long as I'm back by six to treat the Duffus children,' she added more soberly.

'As soon as that? Debbie's out tonight, so I was going to suggest a meal at Tibbie Shiels's Inn. Never mind.'

'We-ell. . .' Lindy was beginning, when a man in his late twenties with a shock of hair the colour of ripe corn came charging round a corner and almost collided with them.

He looked furiously at them, then did a double-take. 'Little Lindy Dunbar—I don't believe it!' He reached out and, grabbing her by the shoulders, he kissed her in a way that once upon a time would have had her swooning. Everybody in her year had had a crush on Michael Sinclair sooner or later. 'And people say there's no deity!' he purred. 'Do you realise I was going to ring you tonight?'

'You were?' Lindy could hardly believe her ears. She cast a quick look round for anybody Michael might be wanting to annoy, but there was only Lyall standing by, wearing a look of disapproval. 'But why?'

'Because I'm just about to start a locum consultancy down your way at the Roxburgh.' Consultancy my foot! thought Lindy. 'So what are you doing in the big city?'

'I've been discussing equipment for our new practice

physio department. But what am I thinking of? I should introduce my father's partner, Lyall Balfour. Lyall — Michael Sinclair. Michael's in Geriatrics.'

The two doctors shook hands with the minimum of enthusiasm before Michael returned to the assault. 'Lindy, my angel, I've got a couple of patients to see and then I'm free for the day, so why not hang around and then we'll go for a drink and do some catching up. There's no need to worry about getting home — I'll drive you down later.'

'Well now——' she began, torn between duty and the pleasant surprise of discovering how much Lyall seemed to disapprove.

He stepped forward and intervened. 'I'm sure Lindy would enjoy catching up with an old acquaintance, but we have to hurry home so that she can treat two patients.'

Michael gave Lyall a shut-up-this-is-none-of-your-business look which had no effect on him whatever. Lyall simply stared him down.

'Surely that's for Lindy to decide?' Michael said less confidently.

'I'd like to take you up on that drink,' said Lindy, 'but Lyall's right. Those children really need their treatment — and I promised.'

'Surely one missed treatment——'

'You'd better believe there's no alternative, Sinclair,' Lyall interrupted implacably. Then he grabbed Lindy's other elbow.

It really was rather nice to be a bone of contention between two such attractive men. Or rather it would have been — had she been able to believe that either of them was serious!

'All right, then, I'll ring you whenever I get down your way. We'll have a lot of fun when I'm working at

the Roxburgh.' Michael then leaned down to kiss her
again; something Lindy made no attempt to avoid.

'Come on,' growled Lyall as Michael walked away.
She was standing there, as though too bemused to do
more than gaze after him. 'Come *along*, Lindy!'

'Sorry. I expect you'd like to avoid the rush-hour
traffic.'

He glared at her. 'After half a lifetime coping with the
London traffic, I hope I can handle anything Edinburgh
has to offer.'

He was marching on at a great pace and Lindy was
having difficulty keeping up in such high heels on the
tiled floor. She was trying to decide whether it would
annoy him more if she didn't mention Michael than if
she did. By the time they reached the car she still hadn't
decided, but once they were in and fastening their
seatbelts he asked with deliberate offhandedness, 'Is he
really an old friend of yours?'

'Michael? I should say so! We go way back.'

'Yet you seem to have lost touch lately.'

Trust him to see the weak spot in the picture she was
trying to paint! 'There didn't seem much point in —
in trying to keep things going after I had to leave
Edinburgh,' she explained.

'Out of sight, out of mind?'

'I suppose so. . .'

'For him or for you?'

Oh, but he was crafty! 'This will no doubt come as a
great surprise to you,' she said coldly, 'but Michael and
Bill are not the only men who think I'm attractive!'

'And in case you don't know it, that one back there is
one of those men to whom *any* woman under forty-five is
attractive! You'd be better sticking with Bill. He's a
thoroughly decent type.'

Damn him — just when she'd been allowing herself to

wonder if he could possibly be jealous! 'I'm sure you mean well,' she ground out, unconsciously echoing words of his to her soon after his arrival. 'But I'm quite capable of choosing my own friends.'

'My sister said something very like that when we tried to get her to see sense about that disastrous husband of hers.'

'And I expect Debbie resented your interference in her affairs as much as I do!'

'If she did, she didn't say so.'

'Because of course *she* knows how wise you are in these matters, whereas I ——'

'What the hell do you mean by that?' He was so steamed up now that he bungled the gear change and swore some more, under his breath.

'Kindly do not swear at me in that vulgar fashion,' said Lindy in her grandest tones. 'I'm not used to it.'

'Then don't make spiteful innuendoes!'

'My, my, we are touchy today! Apparently I've unwittingly hit a sore point. So sorry!' If only I had the least idea what I was talking about. . .

'You sound it, I must say. I'd no idea you could be so bitchy.'

'You don't improve on acquaintance either! Kindly take me straight home and not by the roundabout route.'

'If you hadn't been so taken up with being as unpleasant as possible, you'd have noticed that's exactly what I *am* doing,' he growled.

'I'm beginning to wonder if my joining the practice is such a good idea after all,' Lindy muttered.

'If you don't like it, you can always go back to Edinburgh!'

'I don't want to do that—not now that Michael's landed that job at the District Hospital,' she returned provokingly. She glanced quickly at Lyall. His expression was grim, but he didn't answer.

The rest of the homeward journey was accomplished in uncomfortable silence, and when they got there, Lyall dropped Lindy at the gates of Downside House with only a stilted word or two of thanks for her afternoon of research. Then he drove off as though pursued by fiends.

In her strappy sandals, the gravel of the drive was punishing, and Lindy tried to use the aggravation to whip up anger against Lyall. It didn't work. She was too upset about their quarrel, while at the same time burning with curiosity about what had lain behind his sudden heated outburst. Realising that somehow it had to do with a woman didn't make her feel any better. It was a very subdued Lindy who cycled off to treat the Duffus children not long afterwards.

It had been settled between the girls that Debbie would spend a morning in the surgery with Lindy before taking over next week, so Lindy was at her post on Friday even earlier than usual. Debbie arrived soon after, looking very cool and competent in her crisp white uniform and with her lovely dark hair swept up in a neat roll. 'Right, so what's the drill?' she asked brightly.

'First we look out the records of those already booked in, stopping as necessary to take any calls.'

'Sounds straightforward enough,' reckoned Debbie, and so it was with the two of them to share the chores, and she insisted afterwards that she'd really enjoyed her morning. 'It was a doddle, Lindy.'

'I'm really glad you were here, I can tell you,' said Lindy. 'It's a long time since we had so many dressings in one morning. And all that chaperoning too! Not to mention all the calls and queries.'

'It'll be much easier when they've appointed a secretary, because then——'

'They're never going to sack Mrs Gavin!' cried Lindy with horror.

'Certainly not,' said Lyall, coming into the tiny kitchen and practically flattening them against the walls. 'I've ordered a computer, and as Mrs Gavin wants nothing to do with all that fancy modern electronical stuff, as she calls it, she'll be taking on the reception work, which is much more to her taste. And her motherly presence will be a great comfort to anxious patients.'

He'd made a very good point there, but his manner, so calm and remote in marked contrast to yesterday, was infuriating to one whose heart was banging about in her chest like a steam hammer. 'Why is it that I'm always the last to get to know about these things?' Lindy asked tartly.

'Probably because until recently you've taken very little interest in the reorganisation,' said Lyall, sounding equally tart himself now.

That was true, but how maddening of him to spell it out! 'Have you time to come and talk to the electrician?' he asked. 'He needs to know where you want power points in the treatment-room.'

'Certainly. I wouldn't want to hold up progress. I'll go and get my sketch plan.' She squeezed past him, trying to ignore the feel of him, and sped to the reception desk. Then she followed him in silence across the waiting-room, through the hole in the wall and so into the new building. Debbie would have come too, but Lyall told her that was more than her life was worth. 'If Ellen doesn't get her caffeine fix on time, she'll have the whole place down about our ears,' he said in a softened tone in marked contrast to what had gone before. It was amazing the way he and Ellen had taken to one another.

Yet they're as much chalk and cheese as he and I are, thought Lindy.

Lyall stopped abruptly and she all but cannoned into him. 'I was forgetting—you've not been in here before, have you?' Then before she could confirm that, he all but thrust her into a light and spacious room. 'The new consulting-room.'

'For you,' she assumed.

'No—for your father, if I can persuade him to move. He *is* the senior partner.'

'He says you're all equal.'

'He would—that's the sort of man he is. That's a store-room across the corridor——' he strode on, leaving her to follow '—a new dressing-room for Debbie on this side, the secretary's room, patients' loos and finally your room.'

'What's that open-plan bit for?' asked Lindy.

'Waiting space for your patients. It'll relieve pressure in the main waiting-room and save you a lot of walking up and down to call them in.'

'That was very thoughtful of you,' she said.

'You'll probably be a lot busier than you imagine—and we don't want any wasted time,' he returned, spoiling the effect.

'I certainly hope to earn my salary,' Lindy answered shortly. He was so cool and businesslike today—and she didn't like it.

'Oh, here you are, Tam,' said Lyall in a markedly friendlier tone when the electrician came hurrying towards them.

'Sorry to keep you, pal,' said Tam, 'but I was just finishing a wee job back there.'

'I didn't think you were skiving. Are we all right for the golf tomorrow?'

'I booked us in for eight after you said you wanted to

get out early before the crowd. And if you can come for your lunch after, Marie says you'll be very welcome.'

'Tell her thanks very much,' said Lyall, backing away down the corridor. 'Debs'll be glad to have me out of the way.'

'We're old friends,' explained Tam Dewar in answer to Lindy's astonished expression. 'Lyall and Debbie spent every summer holiday at the manse, ye ken, before old Mr Balfour retired. And the trouble he got Ian and me into! Ian Chisholm — you mind Ian, Lindy — he's an accountant in Glasgow now. All I can say is that if Ian's dad hadn't been the police sergeant we'd all have been detained at Her Majesty's pleasure more than once. Happy days — but about your power points, lassie. You'll be wanting them about a metre up from the floor, I'm thinking.'

'Perfect, Tam. And I've got a sketch here. What do you think?'

Tam thought her suggested layout was just fine, and five minutes later Lindy was back in the surgery. She was getting her father's room ready for her last physiotherapy session before going on holiday when she sensed that she was being watched. She looked round to see Lyall regarding her gravely from the doorway. 'So what have I forgotten to do now?' she asked touchily.

He winced at her tone. 'Nothing that I've noticed. Have you sorted things out with Tam?'

'I have. Tam is very easy to — deal with.' Unlike some, hung implied in the air between them.

'Yes, he's very good at his job,' Lyall agreed impassively. He didn't go. Lindy went on with her preparations. When he cleared his throat, the sound made her jump, on edge as she was.

'I'm off this weekend,' he said awkwardly.

'So am I — to Switzerland.'

'I know — and I'd like to wish you a good holiday now, in case I don't see you before you go.'

'Thank you.'

'You're still angry about yesterday.' It was a statement, not a question. 'All right, so it's probably none of my business, but I——' He cleared his throat again. Lindy had never seen him so ill at ease, his calm manner gone now that there was nobody about who must be deceived. 'The only reason I said what I did was because I'd hate to see you get hurt, that's all.'

'Why?'

He took his time before asking, 'Why not?'

Lindy gave a hiss of pure frustration. 'Look, you manage your affairs and I'll manage mine! Right?'

'He's not the right man for you, you know.'

'How would you know? There's a phrase to describe folk like you,' she burst out. 'Something about dogs — and mangers!' The minute the words were out, she regretted them. She'd as good as told him how she felt about him.

'I deserved that,' he said quietly, 'but it's quite true that I'd hate to see you get hurt — whether you believe it or not.'

There was no denying his sincerity, no matter how baffling his motives. 'I'll try to believe it,' said Lindy.

A self-mocking smile touched his lips for a second.

'That's about all I have any right to expect,' he returned before swinging round abruptly and walking away.

CHAPTER SEVEN

THE train from London was crowded, stuffy and very noisy. Lindy got up and elbowed her way to the door long before the ancient Border town of Berwick-on-Tweed came into view. She opened the window and breathed good clean air for the first time that day. Switzerland had been fun. Her friend had made a lot of interesting new friends, and they'd pulled out all the stops to entertain the girl from Scotland. Even so, she was very glad to be going home. Despite all the holiday diversions, she had returned in memory again and again to that quarrel and then the last brief scene with Lyall before she went away. With things so confused, so fraught between them, it had been the worst possible time to go away. So Lindy was glad to be going home. She couldn't wait to find out how Lyall would react — and she would feel — the next time they met.

Only a handful of passengers left the train at Berwick and all the others had somebody to meet them. The train had been more than an hour late, and now Lindy had missed her bus. She towed her suitcase down the bumpy platform, wondering how long she'd have to wait for the next.

A white Ferrari was parked in the station yard. Its driver was leaning against it, long legs crossed at the ankles, arms folded across his chest, his expression brooding.

'My God — something's wrong with Pa!' breathed Lindy. She abandoned her case and ran forward, heart thumping. 'My father. . .?'

Lyall pushed himself upright, his expression clearing. 'He's fine — away to St Andrews for a few days of golf.'

She stopped three feet away from him. 'Then why——?'

He shrugged. 'I had an errand in Berwick, so Ellen and Debbie agreed I should meet you.' Her cousin and his sister had decided, not him.

'And the train was so late,' she said to his back view as he strode past her to recover her case.

He hoisted it into the boot of the car, giving her a crooked grin. 'I must admit I hadn't bargained for that.'

'And now your Saturday evening is all messed up. . .'

He shrugged again. 'That rather depends on how you look at it.' He opened the passenger door, relieved her of her coat and hand luggage, and tossed them on the back seat. 'Did you enjoy your holiday?' he asked conscientiously when he joined her in the car.

'Yes, thank you. I had a wonderful time.'

'And now it's back to auld clothes and porridge, as they say.'

'East, west, hame's best,' returned Lindy, feeling silly as she said it. Why can I never say clever, impressive things to him? she wondered.

'There's something in that,' he returned as they set off. And then, 'That's a most impressive tan you've collected. And you've had something done to your hair too.'

'There was this marvellous Italian hairdresser who cuts like a dream. You're very observant; I didn't think it was that noticeable.'

'I've been waking up to quite a lot of things lately,' he returned obscurely.

Lindy didn't know what to make of that, shrank from asking him to explain, and played safe by asking how the new surgery was coming along.

She watched his mouth tighten as she spoke. So would he have liked her to follow up that remark? 'Another week or so and we'll be up and running,' he answered neutrally.

'That's wonderful! And how are all my patients?'

'Queueing up impatiently. Debbie will be sorry to hand over the Duffus children—even though Fiona told her she's got a long way to go before she's as expert as you.'

'The cheeky wee besom! I've a good mind not to give her the present I've brought back for her. Talking of Debbie—how is she settling down? Not regretting coming, I hope?' I'm chattering too much, Lindy told herself. How can I get things back on to a personal note?

'Anything but,' said Lyall. 'She did find things a bit hectic at first, but now we've appointed the secretary and Mrs Gavin has taken over reception duties, all's well.'

'That's good. So once she's made a few friends—— What's so funny?' she asked when Lyall laughed briefly.

'I can't imagine how she'd manage to fit in any more,' he said. 'She spends every spare minute with Andy.'

'Well, I'll be——' Lindy was chuckling herself now. 'I bet Elspeth's absolutely seething!' But then again, perhaps not. She sent him a quick sideways glance, willing him to be frank.

'It wouldn't be surprising,' he said. 'She's seen Andy as her own special property for quite some time, I gather.'

So whatever else he'd been doing while she was away, it didn't sound as though he'd been seeing Elspeth. And even if he did have an errand in Berwick and didn't come specially, he did wait all that time. . .'I haven't thanked you properly for meeting me,' Lindy said earnestly. 'It really was extremely kind of you. The bus takes forever.'

'I'm glad it was — welcome.'

'It was — I can't tell you! The train was awful; packed and noisy — and with no dining car, even though there should have been.'

'So when did you last eat?' He sounded concerned.

'On the plane. About half-six this morning.'

'Good grief, you must be starving!'

'Well, I wouldn't say no to a chocolate bar — if you happen to have such a thing.'

'Don't you think stopping for a meal would be more sensible?'

'Have I not held you up enough already tonight?' she queried.

'I have to eat too, my sister's out with her boyfriend and I don't much like cooking,' said Lyall, as he stopped the car in front of the best hotel in Kelso.

'Well, if that's the way it is, I don't mind admitting that I'm absolutely ravenous,' said Lindy.

'But of course. What else but near starvation would have driven you to agree?'

She scanned his face, looking for clues and finding none in his impassive expression. 'If I seemed ungrateful, then I'm sorry, because I'm not. I don't always understand you — in fact, hardly ever — but right now you're being very kind to me, and I really appreciate it. Have I made myself clear?'

'As crystal,' he said, smiling. 'So let's go and find out if this place can live up to its reputation.'

'What'll you have to drink?' he asked as they entered the cocktail bar.

'Something soft, please. I might get tipsy, drinking on an empty stomach, and I'd hate to be an embarrassment.'

Lyall ordered two dry sherries and a large packet of crisps. 'That won't do much damage if you mop it up as you go with these.' He opened the bag and put it in front of her.

Lindy took a handful. 'You can't imagine how good these taste — and thanks for opening the bag. I usually make a muck-up of it and spill half of them.'

'I've never known anybody as ready as you are to proclaim your faults — such as they are,' he told her.

Lindy turned wide, disbelieving eyes on him. 'Do I really do that?'

'More often than you know.'

'Imagine! Still, what's the point of pretending to be perfect when you know damn fine you're not? Folk only think you're conceited.'

'Not everybody sees as clearly as you — or is half as honest.'

'Dear me, you'll have me blushing in a minute,' she said, taking another handful of crisps. But if I see as clearly as you seem to think, how come I find you such a puzzle? she wondered.

She forgot that, though, as the evening progressed. Lyall was being so agreeable that gradually they became almost as easy together as they had been the day of the removal, when the three of them had gone out for supper and met Andy. Lindy wasn't clear why he was making this effort, but she'd not be spoiling things by expecting too much — and showing it! — tonight.

Still sticking with non-controversial things, she decided it was safe to admire his car when they left the hotel after dinner. 'So elegant and powerful,' she said, stroking the shining roof. 'I bet it's a delight to drive.'

'Why not try it and find out?' he suggested.

'You mean you'd trust *me* — anybody — to drive it?'

'You're not anybody,' he said. 'And the answer is yes.'

'I'm absolutely—overcome.' And so she was—and whatever had come over him? 'But I can't. I've not taken my test yet.'

Lyall was astonished. 'I thought everybody drove nowadays.'

'I did start taking lessons just before I came home; having a car would have made it so much easier and quicker getting down to see Pa, but that all went by the board when he had his attack.'

'Presumably you have a provisional licence, then—and I'm pretty sure I've still got the L-plates I used for a friend. . .' Lyall was rummaging in the glove compartment.

'You're never thinking of letting me drive now?' she gasped.

He emerged triumphant. 'Wouldn't you like that?'

'Need you ask? Only I don't have my licence with me—and besides, I'd hate for us to fall out again, now we seem to be getting along quite well. I've only had ten lessons. . .'

'We all have to start somewhere,' said Lyall. 'And at the first sign of discord, we'll stop and change over. How's that?'

'I hope you realise what you're taking on,' she warned when the L-plates were in place and he was opening the driver's door for her. She climbed in and studied the control panel. 'It's worse than Concorde's,' she decided gloomily.

Lyall whistled. 'You didn't tell me you could fly Concorde! This'll be child's play, then.' She giggled, relaxing as he'd intended she should. 'Never mind the flashing lights—most of them are only there for show. The controls are all where you'd expect them to be.'

'I do hope it's not got one of those kangaroo clutches, Lyall.'

He hid a smile and asked, 'Don't all clutches feel that way until one gets used to them?'

'Mm — yes, I dare say. . . I think I'll wait for that bus to move off before I do.'

'A very wise decision,' he agreed gravely, but with a tiny tremor at the corner of his mouth.

'How'm I doing?' Lindy asked cautiously about five minutes later.

'I'm very impressed — so how about changing up into third now?'

'Yes, I think I will.' Having managed that without too much grinding of gears, she asked indignantly, 'Did you see the way that man glared at me as he overtook?'

'Some people soon forget learning themselves.'

'That's very true. Look, I'm doing almost thirty now.'

'That's your reckless streak coming out. Mind that cyclist!'

Lindy slammed on the brakes, bringing them to a dead stop.

'You didn't need to be quite so drastic, my dear.'

'But there's a car coming towards us, so I couldn't have overtaken. Could I?'

It looked about the size of a small biscuit box, and Lyall said, 'There might have been time — but better to err on the safe side. Perhaps you should let all the cars behind you go by before you take off again.'

Lindy counted nine. 'Oh, dear — are you very embar- rassed?' she asked unhappily.

'Not in the least,' he insisted.

'I do think you're so patient and kind.'

'If I'd realised that this was all it took to get that sor of admission from you, I'd have started months ago,' he said ruefully. 'All the same, I'll take over before we get to the house. Those gateposts. . .'

'I understand. Now don't speak to me until I get going again. Mirror, signal, handbrake. . .or is all that for stopping?'

'Do you want me to tell you?'

'No, thank you. I think I know what I'm doing. . .'

'Tell me honestly now, Lyall, how did I do?' Lindy begged to be told when they rolled to a stop in the drive of Downside House, Lyall having driven the last tricky fifty yards or so.

'The first time I took Debbie out, we ended up in a duckpond,' he said, cravenly dodging the question.

'That was unfortunate, but at least I kept to the road, did I not? Well, almost,' she added, remembering a grass verge or two.

'You'll do better next time, little one.'

'You mean—you're actually willing to take me out again?'

'You do want to learn to drive, don't you?' he asked.

'Oh, yes!'

'Then there will be a next time.' He fetched her luggage from the boot and put it in the porch.

Lindy was disappointed that he hadn't said when—like tomorrow—but she mustn't be greedy. They'd come a long way this evening. She unlocked the door and switched on the hall lights. 'I can't thank you enough for this evening,' she said. 'Being met and so well fed—and as for the driving lesson——' She stopped, looking upwards because Lyall was frowning at the silent old house. 'Is anything wrong?'

'I was wondering if you'll be all right,' he said doubtfully. 'Are you sure you don't mind staying here by yourself?'

'What, in sleepy wee Eyretoun? Not in the least. But thanks for asking. You're very thoughtful.'

'I've been told more than once that I improve on acquaintance,' he returned whimsically, toting her case into the hall.

'Have some coffee,' suggested Lindy, loath to let this amazing evening get away from her.

'Thanks, but no, thanks,' he said gently. 'Apart from the fact that you could do with an early night, there's a patient I want to visit this side of midnight.'

'I quite understand.' That was an excuse she would never query. 'Goodnight then, Lyall.' Would he kiss her? Oh, please yes. . .

After what seemed like ages, he leaned down and kissed her gently on the cheek. 'It's nice to have you home again, Lindy. We've all missed you. Now be sure to lock up after me, won't you?'

'I'll do that,' she said expressionlessly. Was there ever such an infuriating man? She was no nearer understanding him than she'd ever been!

On the hall table was a note from her father. After a string of domestic reminders and hoping that she'd enjoyed her holiday, he had written, 'A Dr Mike Sinclair has called several times and is very anxious for you to ring him back at the Roxburgh as soon as possible. Hope there's nothing wrong.' Lindy read the message through again. If Lyall had been just a wee bit more forthcoming just now, she'd not have followed it up. As it was, she'd be phoning Mike tomorrow. Lyall liked her—she was almost sure of that now—but would that liking ever grow into love? If she waited for him to make up his mind about that, she'd be too old to care!

It seemed odd on Monday morning not to skip through breakfast and dash into the surgery to organise the day.

But Lindy was finished with all that, and a ladylike week, with only a few physio patients in the afternoons, lay ahead of her. After that, her treatment-room would be ready and she'd be the full-time practice physio.

Lindy set up the ironing board in her room, and while ironing her holiday clothes she thought about yesterday. She had phoned Mike in the morning and he'd been with her by three. They'd gone for a walk along by the river and had high tea at a wayside inn. Then he'd had to go because he was really on call this weekend and had only got out by browbeating his junior to cover for him. He was coming again tonight and taking her to dinner at the Eyretoun Arms. He had suggested somewhere out of the town, but Lindy had her reasons for wanting to be seen with him on her home territory. With any luck at all, Lyall would get to hear of it. She still hadn't quite given up hope of making him jealous.

The ironing done, Lindy offered to help Meg with some of the bigger cleaning jobs, but Meg didn't want Lindy getting under her feet. 'Away with you to the kitchen and bake something,' she instructed.

So when Debbie came through at half-past eleven Lindy was taking scones out of the oven. 'That's me done for the morning,' said Debbie, 'so I thought I'd come and have my coffee with you. Shall I put on the kettle?'

'Please — go right ahead.' Lindy frowned at a few burnt currants and picked them off, singeing her fingers.

'We were all very disappointed that you couldn't come to supper last night,' said Debbie, when they were sitting opposite one another, nursing steaming mugs of coffee. She didn't specify who all 'they' were. 'Can I have a piece of that shortbread?' She helped herself before Lindy could answer.

'I was sorry too,' said Lindy. 'But my friend ——'

'Quite. Who is he, anyway? Don't bother to answer that! The real question is, does he matter?'

Her directness would come across as downright rudeness in anybody else, Lindy reflected. 'I've known him for years and he says he's taken this job at the District Hospital to be near me, but I'm not absolutely sold on that,' she told Debbie.

Debbie frowned. 'Lyall seems to think differently. I do hope he's not going to get hurt again.'

Again? What did Debbie mean? Suddenly Lindy remembered what she'd said after Elspeth called at the flat on moving day. How had she put it? Oh, yes. I'd have thought he'd had enough of her sort. But now Debbie was looking rueful, almost guilty, as though she knew she'd been letting her tongue run away with her. So any attempt to find out what lay behind that remark would have to be very subtle if it were to be successful.

'Have a scone,' offered Lindy, and then while Debbie was buttering it she began, 'You said just now that you hoped Lyall wasn't going to be hurt again. What did you mean, Debbie?' Oh, very subtle, she thought, but then subtlety was never my strong point.

Debbie bit her lip. 'I expect I meant his having to give up surgery. That hit him very hard. He'd never wanted to do anything else since he was quite a little boy.'

So if she had been referring to a woman, as Lindy had surmised, Debbie wasn't going to say. There was something else, though. 'Somehow, I'd got the idea you thought that I might — hurt Lyall. Silly of me. How could I?'

Debbie must be regretting hinting that too, because she said quickly, 'That was just me and my over-ripe imagination. Lyall does like you, though — and I couldn't help thinking how splendid it would be if you two were to fall in love and live happily ever after. Only things never turn out the way one would like, have you noticed?' she asked, finishing on a question as she often did.

Lindy tried the same technique. 'And how do you see things turning out for yourself, Debs?'

'Oh, lord, I've no idea,' shrugged Debbie, but she was smiling as she said it, and looking very complacent.

There's one romance that's obviously got off to a good start, thought Lindy wistfully. But then they're both such straightforward and uncomplicated people.

At lunchtime it was Ellen's turn to visit. Lindy was just sitting down to a sandwich, but she pushed the plate across the table to her cousin and made herself another.

'Good holiday, Lindy?' asked Ellen with her mouth full.

'Wonderful, thanks. And I'm so glad you got Pa to see sense and take a wee break.'

'That was Lyall's doing. He's a wonder, that lad. His coming here was the best thing that could have happened — for all of us.' Ellen was very sure of that.

Lindy hoped Ellen was right, but from her own point of view it was too soon, or too risky, to agree. 'Were you busy this weekend, Ell?' she asked to change the subject.

'You've lost count while you've been away,' said Ellen with one of her cackles. 'This was Lyall's weekend on, not mine.'

'But he came to meet me!'

'Yes. When he suggested it, we all agreed it was a good idea, so I said I'd do the evening for him——' another cackle ' — just so long as he did a Cinderella and got back into harness by midnight. Us oldies need our sleep, you know.'

So that was why he didn't stay for coffee. Why couldn't he have said? Lindy wondered. Because he wanted me to think he had an errand and hadn't made the trip solely for my benefit. But if I had known, then I'd not have phoned Mike. . .

'Am I getting any coffee?' demanded Ellen loudly.

'Yes, of course. We'd better be quick, though. I have to get started soon.'

Mrs Turnbull was big with news today. 'The Robertsons are very pleased,' she announced. 'They were awful scared the Hamilton woman would get Andy, and we all know she's no better than she should be.'

'How did you get here today?' asked Lindy, having noticed that her patient had had the first of her distorted big toes operated on.

'My sister drove me down and she's waiting, so I hope you'll be quick. Is she making any progress?'

'I don't know, Mrs Turnbull. Your sister's not a patient of mine.'

The postmistress clucked impatiently at Lindy for being such a dimwit. 'I meant Elspeth Hamilton — with the new doctor. He was seen talking to her again yesterday — in the *street*, as bold as brass!'

'Imagine that, but perhaps we'd better get started as you're in such a hurry let's give you your electrical treatment for the foot-in-waiting. And after that I'll see if I can't get you walking better. You'll get a bad back if you hirple about like that.'

Mrs Johnstone the bank manager's wife was next here to have some soothing deep-heat treatment for her recurrent lumbago. Miss Calder, the piano teacher, had occupation-related muscular rheumatism in her neck and shoulders and was as tense as iron, and Geordie Burns had come to have skin grafts on his leg massaged with lanolin, after his latest escapade.

Fiona came in last today, and very late. 'Thank heaven!' cried Lindy thankfully when she appeared. '

was getting really worried.' The child had obviously been crying. 'What's wrong, darling?'

Fiona ran to Lindy and hid her face against her soft bosom. 'I was fretting all day about ma wee brother,' came the muffled reply. 'And teacher said I was wool-gathering and she kept me in!'

Which meant that Fiona had missed the school bus and had had to tote her heavy school-bag from one side of town to the other. I'll be having something to say to that teacher! Lindy decided grimly. 'So Calum's not so well, then, pet,' she said gently as she stroked the child's lank fair hair.

Calum, it transpired, had had another of his digestive upsets. Granny had said it was the beginning of the end and had them all thoroughly upset by the time lovely Dr Balfour arrived. He had quickly sussed out the trouble and took Gran into the kitchen, where he read her the riot act. As a result, she had stormed off home, vowing never to come and help them out again. 'So as ma daddy says, there's aye a silver lining,' ended Fiona, looking a little brighter at the thought.

Lindy then handed over the present she'd brought: a prettily carved and painted weather-house. Not a lot of use as a barometer, judging by the way the two little figures swayed in and out at random, but Fiona was delighted with it. 'And did you bring anything for Calum?' she asked. Lindy had brought him some chocolate animals, but they agreed to keep them until he had recovered from his setback.

Lyall returned from his visits just as Fiona was leaving. He promptly scooped her up, dumped her in the car and took her home. Lindy hung about, taking her time about tidying the consulting-room in the hope of still being there when he returned. She just happened to be making tea at the time. 'Would you like some?' she asked casually.

'I'd love some, if it's no trouble.'

She carried the tray to his room. 'I was really sorry I couldn't come to supper yesterday,' she said, 'but by the time Debbie rang I'd made other arrangements.'

'That was my fault,' he said. 'I said you'd probably be tired after your journey, so she decided not to disturb you too early.' He grinned at her suddenly, disturbingly. 'I'd had it in mind to give you another driving lesson — patients permitting.'

'And I'd much have preferred that to — to. . .' But she no longer wanted him to know she'd been with Mike.

He didn't press her. 'I'm on call again tonight, but you could still have that lesson — there being a phone in the car.'

'Oh, dear, I've arranged to meet somebody,' she wailed.

Her obvious disappointment pleased him. 'Perhaps I'd better get myself on tomorrow's list before somebody else does,' he said.

'Yes, please,' Lindy said eagerly.

'You're very keen to learn to drive,' he said experimentally.

'But of course! Especially as you're such a good and patient teacher.'

'Thanks for the testimonial,' he said with one of those crooked little smiles she loved so much.

'You deserve it,' she insisted. Their eyes met in a lengthy glance; questioning, probing, significant. But of course the phone had to ring and spoil things.

Mike was early, and as Lindy wasn't quite ready she asked him in and settled him in the sitting-room with a sherry while she went to finish her make-up.

He whistled long and slow when she reappeared in the dress Lyall had said was too old for her, then he looked her up and down in a way she found made her rather uncomfortable. She expected an extravagant compliment after that, but he said instead, 'I imagine your father's out on a call.'

'No, he's away for a few days.'

He looked thoughtful. 'Leaving you all alone in the house with the new partner? I can't say I approve of that. But perhaps you have a housekeeper. . .'

'No — and Lyall shares a flat with his sister.'

'So you're here on your own?' queried Mike.

'Yes, but I'm not bothered. We don't get many burglaries in Eyretoun,' Lindy assured him.

'All the same, you should keep the door locked between house and surgery. There are always the decadent few on the look-out for drugs.'

'Yes, I know — and I do keep the door locked,' said Lindy, feeling relieved, yet not sure why. What else could he have been thinking of, if not her safety?

The evening went as well as yesterday. Mike was so amusing — and attentive. Gradually the feeling that he was only bothering with her because she was the only girl he knew down here began to recede.

'Coffee in the lounge, sir,' said the waiter at the end of their meal.

Mike glanced through the dividing doors. 'But the lounge is packed,' he noticed. 'Would you think it very cheeky of me if I suggested coffee over at your place instead?'

Lindy looked too and realised he wasn't exaggerating. 'It looks to me as though we haven't any choice,' she agreed lightly.

'That's my girl!' approved Mike with a positive leer.

She hoped he wasn't going to be a nuisance, but she could hardly change her mind now.

'Can I help?' he asked, following her into the kitchen when they got back to the house.

'You could take some cups off the dresser.'

'Consider it done. This reminds me of that party at Conn Dwyer's place. You remember. . .' He reminisced easily and amusingly for as long as it took the coffee to brew, then carried the tray along to the sitting-room.

Lindy frowned when he helped himself to her father's brandy before she could offer it, but didn't get really uneasy until he reached for the decanter a third time. Add that to goodness knows how many sherries and almost a whole bottle of wine. . . 'Steady on, Mike,' she said mildly. 'You're driving, remember, and the police around here are hot stuff on catching folk who are over the limit.'

'Who says I'm going back tonight?' he asked softly, leaning towards her.

They were sitting side by side on the couch, and now Lindy leapt up as though stung by hornets. 'Now look here——' she began firmly.

'You couldn't agree fast enough when I suggested coming back here,' Mike said dangerously.

'Coffee is not an automatic invitation to hop into bed,' she said, backing towards the door.

He got up with surprising speed for a man of his size and state of intoxication. 'Bloody little tease!' he snarled. 'Always were. Well, now it's payday!'

His first lunge tore the flimsy dress from shoulder to hem. He was between her and the door, so Lindy made for the window. He brought her down with a clumsy rugby tackle, and they rolled together on the floor. She beat at him uselessly with her fists, scratching his face and pulling at his wrists, desperate to stop him ripping off her clothes or unzipping his own. Rage had given way now to a terror that threatened to paralyse her. With one last effort, she screamed at the top of her lungs and reached out, hoping to topple the standard lamp and knock him out. But it fell the wrong way and knocked over a table with a resounding crash that shook the room.

Oh, God, she was pinned to the floor by his weight, and his filthy hands were everywhere. She tried to scream again, but the sound was pitifully thin. . .

Lindy was almost fainting with fear when suddenly Mike was lifted up bodily and she heard a loud thwack! Soon after came a sound like a heavy sack being thrown on to the gravelled drive, an angry shout and then the slamming and bolting of the front door. She struggled to a sitting position, trembling violently. She screamed and cowered back at the sound of a man's footsteps approaching, whimpered when she was scooped up in strong arms, and subsided weeping in the boneless aftermath of fear when she realised who was holding her.

She clung to Lyall like a limpet, clutching great handfuls of his shirt and burying her face in his shoulder from relief and shame. He held her tight, his hands strong yet soothing, his voice low and gentle as he uttered wordless endearments.

When he would have relaxed his hold to pour her some brandy, she gave a stifled cry and burrowed closer. So he lifted her bodily off her feet and sat down with her in the biggest chair. She curled up in his lap while he rocked her gently, head to head, his lips bestowing gentle kisses.

Bit by bit, Lindy grew calmer, stopped whimpering and stopped trembling. 'He said — it was all my fault. . .'

'They always do,' he whispered back.

'But *you* don't think ——'

'I know it wasn't — because I know you.' His lips on her bruised mouth were gentle, like balm. 'My poor darling little innocent,' he murmured.

'He didn't — didn't. . .'

His arms tightened convulsively around her. 'I know. I'd have killed him if he had.' The naked savagery of his tone left no room for doubt.

'I did try ——'

'I know that.' She could feel him relaxing again. He took her hand and examined the nails. There was blood and skin underneath. 'I'd give a lot to know how he'll explain away those scratches. It's a pity you couldn't have got him — somewhere else.'

'By the time I realised that's what I ought to do, it was too late,' she explained. 'He'd come at me like a rugby forward.'

'My darling girl ——' Lyall breathed unsteadily.

Lindy began to savour a welcome and wonderful truth. 'I think you're nearly as shocked as I am — was.' With each new proof of his feeling for her she was growing calmer by the minute.

'That was just about the worst moment of my life,' he assured her.

As bad as the accident — and perhaps the other calamity mentioned by his sister but never by him. . . 'It was a miracle you came,' she breathed with another violent shudder as she realised just how much of a miracle. Another second, five at the most. . . She pressed against him again and read his response in the increased pressure of his arms. 'Why did you come?'

'I was working at home and found I'd left some papers I wanted in the surgery. When I heard the crash and heard you scream, I tried the connecting door, but it was locked. I don't remember coming round to the front or anything else, until I — but the rest you know. I knew that swine wasn't to be trusted,' he ground out savagely.

And I thought you were so cool and self-contained, my darling, she thought tenderly, watching his face, dark with fury.

She let her head settle on his shoulder again and they stayed like that, close and silent for some time. Then Lyall said gently, 'I think you're ready for the next stage of the cure.'

'I don't know what you mean,' she said doubtfully.

He kissed her gently. 'A hot bath, a sleeping pill and bed.'

'I don't want to go to bed. I don't want to be alone!'

'You won't be; I'm staying. You can lock your door if you want.'

'Don't be silly,' she whispered. 'I'm not afraid of you.'

'I shall take that as a compliment,' he said. 'Now upstairs with you.'

Lindy undressed quickly, stuffing her clothes into a plastic bag and dropping it out of the window. Then she soaked and scrubbed energetically, to rid herself of the memory of her attacker's greedy hands.

Lyall brought her hot milk and two small white capsules which she swallowed without question. 'Don't you want to know what you're taking, darling?' he queried gently.

'I trust you,' she returned simply.

'Please God you'll never have reason not to,' he murmured half to himself. 'Goodnight, my precious one. I'll not be far away.'

CHAPTER EIGHT

LINDY woke next morning when Lyall brought her breakfast. She sat up, rubbing her eyes, watched him cross the room, then held out her arms like a child.

He put the tray on the end of the bed and sat down to enfold her, kissing her very differently from the comforting way of the night before. 'It's a damn good thing I've got a surgery in ten minutes,' he murmured.

Downstairs, Meg was already crashing about and singing in her usual strenuous and tuneless way. 'Now there's a difficulty,' guessed Lindy when she'd recovered from being kissed so wonderfully, so early in the day.

'Not at all. She's quite happy with the explanation of a twenty-four-hour bug—picked up abroad, of course. Meg doesn't think much of anywhere south of the Border.' Lyall looked thoughtful. 'Mind you, she might not have swallowed that if she'd found your bag of clothes in the flowerbed under your window!'

Lindy looked self-conscious. Last night's gesture of revulsion seemed melodramatic now. 'When did you find them?' she asked.

'Last night. When I went out to hide my car in the garage.' He didn't say he'd also wanted to make sure the aggressor had gone. 'I put them in the boot—where I also put my sheets this morning.'

'You've thought of everything,' she marvelled. 'Have you had much experience of this sort of thing?'

'Certainly not! Still, you'd expect me to say that even if I had.' He stopped grinning and looked thoughtful. 'But Eyretoun is a very small place, so——'

Tenderly she smoothed back a strand of hair that had strayed forward. 'You're not such a townie after all, my love.'

'Underneath the veneer, there was always this simple country boy struggling to get out,' he claimed humorously.

Lindy chuckled. 'He took his time about it. What kept him?'

The wary look she'd thought never to see again was back, but only for a moment before he grinned and said, 'The reason seems absurd now.'

'Tell me,' she urged gently.

'One day perhaps—not now. Anyway, it's no longer important.' Reluctantly he unwound her arms from round his neck and got to his feet. 'Eat your breakfast and have a nice lazy morning—doctor's orders! I'll be back to see my patient later.'

She let him get to the door before she said, 'Lyall—darling—thanks for everything.'

'It was all as much for me as for you,' he answered with a serious intensity.

I've never been so happy in all my life as I am now, she thought, as she picked up her spoon.

Lindy was sitting at the kitchen table reading *The Scotsman* when Debbie came through to the house after surgery. 'So you've recovered,' she said with satisfaction.

She could hardly have missed her brother's absence the night before, but which explanation had he given her? A twenty-four-hour bug or the post-trauma of attempted rape? 'I'm very resilient,' said Lindy—a reply that would do for either.

'How about a coffee?'

'I really came to see if you were well enough to work

or whether you'd like me to cancel your patients, but if you're making some anyway. . .

'Always glad of some company,' said Lindy.

'Aren't we all?' asked Debbie artlessly.

'Yes, how is Andy?' asked Lindy, seizing the initiative.

'Absolutely lovely! Do you know——?' Debbie was beginning when Lyall came in, looking for them both.

'Ellen can't find her list of visits, Debs, so you'd better go through and make her another,' he said from the doorway, where he was holding the door wide open.

'Why do I suddenly have this feeling that I'm wished elsewhere?' she wondered. 'And just as the kettle's boiling, too! I'll come back and see you some time when you're free, Lindy,' she added in a pathetic little voice, going out and shutting the door very pointedly.

Lindy was laughing. 'Has Ellen really lost her list?' Lyall fixed her with a look of outraged innocence. 'Of course she's lost it! Would I lie to the two most important women in my life?'

'There, there!' cried Lindy, running over to him and stroking him soothingly.

'I'm no poodle,' he said, pulling her roughly into his arms and kissing her masterfully.

'You can say that again!' she agreed breathlessly as soon as she could. 'You're being very positive this morning. Will you be keeping it up?'

His hold on her tightened as he said, 'There's nothing like a bit of competition and a damn good fright to show a man his true feelings, young woman. But, delicious as you are, I've simply got to get on with the job. Have you any patients coming this afternoon?'

'A few—why?'

'Because I don't have a surgery this evening, so once I've done my visits——'

'I could be free by five,' she told him.

'Only five and a half hours to wait, then,' he calculated. 'I think I can survive that long.' His eyes roamed hungrily over her face. 'Can I really be this lucky?' he wondered on a murmur. 'I don't believe there's an ounce of spite or selfishness in your make-up.' He kissed her again and was gone, leaving Lindy very thoughtful.

That last remark had sounded as though he were comparing her with somebody. But who? I love him so much, yet I know so little about him, she realised.

Geordie Burns came in soaked and filthy that afternoon; a state he explained away by claiming to have fallen in a puddle. As it hadn't rained for a fortnight and the ground was baked hard, that was obviously untrue. 'You've been mucking about in the river,' accused Lindy. 'Just look at the state of you! You're supposed to keep those grafts clean and dry. Supposing they were to get infected?'

'What's infected mean, miss?' asked Geordie curiously.

'You'll find out fast enough if you don't mend your ways, my lad! Any more of this carry-on and you'll land back in the hospital and have to go through the whole thing again. Only next time it'll be a lot worse!'

Geordie went very pale under all the grime, and Lindy hoped the message had gone home. Cleaning him up more than doubled the length of his treatment, and Miss Calder began to worry about being late for her next pupil. 'This is as bad as the hairdressers',' she muttered.

Not quite, Lindy answered in her mind, as she sent Geordie on his way with another dreadful warning. There, you'd have to pay to be kept waiting. 'Ready for you now, Miss Calder. I do hope the massage is helping.' A few exploratory passes over her patient's neck and

Lindy was able to say, 'Yes, I think it must be. Your muscles are much less tense today.'

Lyall was still out on his rounds by the time Fiona had had her treatment, so Lindy hoisted her on to her bike and pushed her home. Calum was better today. Unlike his sister, the poor wee scrap had lesions in his intestines as well as in his lungs, and so was even frailer than she in consequence. His mother said he was needing a right good professional bashing, but his residual queasiness meant frequent stops, and when Lindy eventually got home, Lyall was just driving out at the gate.

He stopped, got out, seized her bike and stuck it behind the bushes. 'Good! I thought I was going to have to go without you.'

'Go where?' she queried.

'An emergency call somewhere up country. Get in.'

She obeyed. 'But is Ellen not——?'

'Yes, but this won't keep until after surgery. And as we'd have been swanning round the country anyway——' He passed her a slip of paper. 'Do you know how to find this place?'

'Take the Melrose road and after about two miles, turn left by a ruined doocot. But those cottages up by the old quarry are just ruins. I wonder who can be living there?'

'Whoever it is has one very sick child in the throes of an acute asthmatic attack, by the sound of it,' Lyall answered grimly, opening up the Ferrari with a roar as soon as they were clear of the town. When they reached the turning, he swung the car off the road and launched it up the rough moorland track with all the speed and panache of a rally driver. 'What a dump!' he observed as the tumbledown cottages came into view.

Some thin, bedraggled-looking hens ran squawking

into a small patch of kale as he skidded to a halt at the door in a cloud of dust. A young woman came out and cast a withering glance over the powerful car. Lyall forestalled comment by saying succinctly how useful it was for getting him to emergencies in a hurry, like now. 'I'm Dr Balfour. Where's the boy?'

'In here.' She led the way into a dingy bedroom where the child sat hunched over his knees, gasping for breath. 'What are you giving him? We don't believe in drugs,' she muttered as Lyall produced a syringe and a small phial.

'Except cannabis, of course,' he retorted crisply. So that's what I'm smelling, realised Lindy, as she watched him with mute admiration.

'Do you want your child helped or not?' he demanded, syringe at the ready. 'There's not much time. Look at him!'

'Well. . .' Lyall took that for assent, and after a quick preliminary dab with a sterile swab he plunged the needle into the child's arm.

'He's no better,' said the woman, almost before the needle was withdrawn.

'Give it time,' ordered Lyall, in the same uncompromising manner he'd adopted from the first.

'You're a bully!' accused the woman.

'Faced with prejudice and ignorance in a case of life and death — yes!'

But the boy's convulsive gasps were lessening, and his mother could see it. 'I can look after him now,' she said dismissively.

'Where's your husband?' asked Lyall.

'He's not my husband. We're not bothered about little bits of paper.'

'But he is the boy's father?' She nodded. 'Then I want to talk to him as well.'

'You'll have to wait, then. He had to go to the crossroads to phone.'

And against your wishes, I'll bet, thought Lindy. The child began to cough and she hurried to help him. 'Lyall—a sample bottle——'

But he had it ready for her almost as soon as she spoke. She caught a globule of sputum and swiftly recapped the bottle. Lyall took it and held it out for the mother to see. 'Your child has a severe chest infection which probably triggered his asthmatic attack,' he told her. 'This sample will be sent for analysis, after which he'll be given the appropriate antibiotic,' he explained, daring her to refuse.

She gave him an exasperated glance before crossing to the grimy window. 'He's coming now, so you can tell that to him,' she said, apparently passing the buck.

Capitalising on the man's obvious relief when he saw the child's improvement, Lyall firmly advanced the need for hospital treatment. This revived the mother's hostility, but she was overruled for the second time that day, and soon they were bouncing back down the rutted track with father and son in the back of the car. Scorning the dirty threadbare blankets, they had wrapped the boy in Lyall's car rugs.

It was well past seven by the time all the formalities were completed and Lyall rejoined Lindy in the car. She'd waited there on his advice. Neither of them had mentioned Mike, but he'd been in both their minds—and both of them had seen all they wanted to of him.

'All right, Lindy?' Lyall asked immediately.

'As the proverbial rain. Where's the father?'

'He's staying with the child till he goes to sleep.' He got into the car, wrinking his nose distastefully. 'Phew, what a stink!'

'Isn't it just? And I've had all the windows open too.

A telephone's not the only mod con they're lacking in that ruin.'

'I wonder how healthy the other children are?' wondered Lyall. The woman had seen them off with two pale-faced toddlers clinging to her skirts.

'You don't really think Homespun Hattie will let you in to find out, do you?' asked Lindy.

He chuckled at her description. 'We'll bypass her and deal with the father. Something tells me he's had something of a change of heart today.'

'Nothing like a good fright for showing folk the light,' she agreed. Hadn't he said something very like that to her only that morning? 'Now what?' she added as they set off.

'We find a nice little pub and have ourselves some supper,' he said firmly. 'Do you realise it's now nearly eight?'

'No—but I suppose it must be. There's a nice little place called the Watermill in a bend of the Tweed, just a few miles on the road to home. They do a lovely mixed grill there.'

'Who needs the *Good Food Guide* when he's got you?' wondered Lyall as he pointed the car in the right direction.

'How original you are,' she considered. 'No boring old compliments from you about my beautiful eyes or my wonderful figure. So refreshing!'

'As you know perfectly well that you've got beautiful eyes and a wonderful figure, there's no need for me to tell you, is there?'

'Are you ever stuck for the smart retort?' she wondered.

'More often than I'd like,' he claimed.

'I've never noticed it.'

'Could be my luck is changing, then.'

'Did it need to?' she asked. And now she was being serious, not flippant.

'Dear heart, you don't know the half of it,' he returned in comi-tragic accents. Yes, he sounded joky and he was smiling, but he was quite right. She didn't know the half of it. If only she could rid herself of this idea that there was something — some hangover from the past — that was bugging him still.

But was she just being silly? After all, didn't nearly everyone have some scarring experiences in their past? Life wasn't roses all the way for anybody. And if there is something he's certainly concealing it well now, Lindy had to concede as the evening proceeded. She had never known him so relaxed and easy. Now it was impossible to imagine there had ever been a time when she felt anything but completely at ease with him.

When they left the Watermill, Lyall put the L-plates on the car again.

'You're quite serious about this driving business, then,' she said.

He squinted at her over the bonnet. 'Aren't you?'

'Oh, yes. Only folk don't usually learn on high-performance cars like this.'

'If you can master this, then you'll have no trouble coping with any other model,' he explained.

'I get it. Nothing like starting at the top and working down.'

'That rather depends on what you're talking about, but it's not a bad rule in this case.'

When they were ready to set off, Lindy said, 'I've got a friend — you met her the day we went to Edinburgh. Anyway, Jeannie says it's the greatest compliment if a man lets a girl drive his car. With men thinking the way they do about women drivers, that is.'

'But you're going to be a perfect driver,' said Lyall.

He leaned over to kiss the lobe of her ear and whisper, 'Cars don't start unless you switch on the ignition, sweetie.'

'Damn! I knew there must be something I'd forgotten to do. Anyway, how do you know what sort of a driver I'll be?'

'Because I'm teaching you. Why else?'

'You're not short on conceit, are you?' she laughed.

'Knowing one's abilities is not a matter of conceit, but pretending not to is false modesty.'

'I'm beginning to wonder if you're not a bit too clever and clear-sighted for me,' said Lindy with sly irony.

'I wouldn't worry about it. You're fairly clever and clear-sighted yourself.'

'Ooh, lovely! Another compliment to go with the one about being a mine of information on places to eat.'

He reached out to ruffle her hair, changed his mind and kissed her instead. 'Oh, get on with your driving,' he said. 'And if you don't frighten me too much I might manage to think up another nice compliment before we get home.'

When they got to Eyretoun, Lyall told Lindy to drive on past the town green. 'I think we ought to call on Homespun Hattie again. She's bound to be worrying about the boy.'

'All right.' Lindy gritted her teeth and carried on. Slowly. 'I'm very glad to be clear of all that traffic,' she breathed with relief when they were out of the town again. They'd met four cars, a parked van and an old man wobbling about on a bicycle.

'It's certainly heavier than usual tonight,' Lyall agreed, biting on a smile.

She contrived to give him a glance of reproach without taking her eyes off the road for more than a second. 'It's getting late and I was scared we would meet some drunken drivers. They're so unpredictable.'

'So are some of the sober ones.'

'Are you by any chance referring to me?' she demanded.

'Certainly not — you're doing remarkably well tonight. But why did you swerve just then?'

'There was a poor little dead rabbit in the road.'

'But if it was dead ——'

'Going over it again would be like killing it twice,' Lindy explained.

'I didn't think there was anyone quite as sweet as you anywhere in the world,' Lyall said huskily. Which certainly beat anything else he'd said to her so far tonight.

By the time they reached the moorland cottage, the family had gone to bed.

'I was asleep,' said the mother reproachfully when she eventually came frowning and yawning to answer their knock.

Lyall shrugged. 'We thought you might be anxious about your boy.'

'Why? He was better before you took him away. Besides, Jake phoned.'

'How? You don't have a phone.'

'He phoned the police and they sent a man up an hour ago. I hope you're not going to make a nuisance of yourself. We're not into conventional medicine — I told you.'

Lindy gasped aloud, while Lyall retorted evenly, 'Or into conventional good manners either, it seems. As I said, we thought you might be anxious. We should have realised on previous showing that that wasn't very likely!'

'That was telling her,' said Lindy admiringly as they returned to the car.

'In one ear and out the other,' he supposed philosophically. 'But never mind, I feel better for saying it.' He watched her climb into the passenger seat. 'Have you had enough driving for today?'

'I don't fancy tackling that rough road now it's nearly dark. Do you mind?'

'I never mind a show of common sense,' he said. 'What a pity I can't prescibe some for Homespun Hattie!' They were still chuckling about that when they reached the main road and headed back to Eyretoun.

'Coffee?' asked Lindy as the car rolled to a stop at the front door of Downside House.

'Have you ever known me to refuse?' Lyall asked softly. 'Especially if it's accompanied by your wonderful biscuits.'

'So that's why you've been making up to me just lately,' she riposted. 'It's only because I can cook.'

'I'm not going to deny that,' he said, getting out of the car when she did.

'What a disappointment! I hoped you had — another reason.'

'I have. You're also a good little physio — and shaping up to be a good chauffeuse too. See how I like to keep the staff sweet?'

'Fine — so long as it's understood that I'm only putting up with you because you're my father's partner and one of the bosses.'

'But of course,' he purred in her ear, while nibbling at the lobe as well. He did it so neatly that she was bound to wonder how much practice he'd had. Besides, wondering took her mind off the daft, wilting way he was making her feel. 'I'll not be long with the coffee,' she promised briskly.

'Forget the ruddy coffee,' he said, kicking the door shut behind him and taking her in his arms.

Lindy went eagerly, her lips parting to fit with his, clinging, melting. Last night, a man had tried to rape her and she'd fought like a tiger. But tonight. . . She strained closer, exulting in his unmistakable response.

On the upstairs landing a light snapped on and they broke apart as her father appeared at the top of the stairs. 'Lindy? Is that you?' he called down.

'Pa! I thought you weren't coming back until tomorrow.'

'I wasn't, but Tom had to get back to Edinburgh tonight to deal with a family crisis, so I left too — to save him taking the train.' He started down the stairs, pausing when Lyall switched on the hall light. He was surprised and he was showing it.

'Lyall is teaching me to drive,' said Lindy quickly, at the same time as Lyall said he supposed he'd better be getting along.

With her father coming on down the stairs instead of going back to bed, Lindy supposed he had a point. 'I'll see you out,' she whispered.

'How is she shaping up?' asked Dr Dunbar.

'As a driver? Very well.' Lyall looked helplessly from father to daughter. With her father's hand on her shoulder, she looked as though she was under arrest.

Lyall grinned at her in resignation. 'Goodnight, then, Lindy. Goodnight, John.'

'Goodnight, my boy — and thank you. It's really very kind of you to take the trouble.' It was Dr Dunbar who shut and locked the door after Lyall. Then he kissed his daughter and suggested she should tell him all about Switzerland over a nice cup of cocoa.

'If you like, Pa,' she agreed, contriving not to let her frustration show. This is not at all what I had in mind for the next wee while, she thought, as she led the way to the kitchen. She began to chatter about her holiday and kept it up until they were sitting at the kitchen table with a mug of cocoa apiece. Then because she knew her father was far more curious about things nearer home, she asked, 'Isn't it kind of Lyall to let me practise my driving on his lovely car? He was amazed when he found out I'd never taken the test. Of course, he's got the time, being on his own so much now that Debbie's so taken up with Andy.'

'Lyall's no fool. I knew he'd soon see through Elspeth,' said her father.

So, just as she'd suspected, he thought Lyall had transferred his interest to her. Well, hadn't he? And, since it would be really short-sighted of him to tangle with his partner's daughter unless he was sincere, wasn't it time to stop wondering? Probably his initial hesitation had been nothing more than prudence because he had to be sure. Lindy wondered why she'd never seen it that way before; it made such good sense. 'There was never anything in that,' she said confidently. 'Just Elspeth, running after any new man as usual. But you haven't told me about your holiday yet, Pa.'

His curiosity was satisfied now, though, so Dr Dunbar said that would keep until tomorrow and it was high time they were both in their beds.

'I've had a wonderful idea,' said Debbie when she came looking for Lindy after surgery next morning. 'The building is finished, all the equipment and stuff will be in by Saturday and then it's all hands to the pumps, getting straight. So why don't we have a do on Sunday evening when it's all done? Just wine and nibbles for the staff and perhaps people like the community nurses? Nothing elaborate; there isn't time. What do you say?'

'I never say no to a party, so you're on,' agreed Lindy enthusiastically. 'And as there's no time like the present. . .' She rummaged around for pencils and paper. 'Right, guest list first. Ready?'

The partners when told also thought it a splendid idea and gave the girls the go-ahead. As Debbie said on Saturday afternoon, as they all feverishly hung curtains and put things in cupboards, it was only the thought of the grand christening next day that was keeping them going.

It was a terrific success. The two community nurses were the first outsiders to arrive and the doctors were still checking the drugs cupboard after transferring the stock to the new dressing-room. Also invited were the lady who cleaned the surgery, the local chemist, the police sergeant and a representative from the nearest ambulance depot. 'Mustn't leave out anybody who helps us,' Lindy had said.

Mrs Gavin, their typist-turned-receptionist, got rather drunk and very giggly, and Pauline, the new secretary, offered to see her safely home. Lindy had worried that Mrs Gavin might resent the high-tech Pauline, straight out of commercial college, but fortunately they had taken to one another right away.

Eventually, only the doctors, Debbie and Lindy were left. It was getting on for nine and everybody was rather hungry, but disinclined to do anything about it.

'I knew exactly how it would be,' crowed Debbie,' and I've laid on a nice surprise for you, so round to the flat with the lot of you. Right?'

Nobody dissented, and at the flat they found Andy at the kitchen stove, looking very domestic in one of Debbie's aprons. 'You're late,' he said. 'I hope it's not all spoiled.'

Debbie danced across the kitchen to kiss him. 'Only half an hour or so, you darling old grouch. Anyway, all you had to do was to keep things warm. Now then—into the dining-room, everyone—but don't let that fool you. You're only getting canteen-style food.'

Lyall took one end of the table with Ellen and Lindy on either side, while Debbie sat at the other end, between Andy and Dr Dunbar. Canteen-style, she'd said, but what she gave them was mushroom soup, a perfect shepherd's pie and orange mousse as light as air.

'And all I'd expected was bread and cheese,' said Lindy's father, summing up for them all.

'Now you know why I was so keen to import my sister,' said Lyall when nobody had been able to refuse a second helping of pudding.

'And here was I thinking it was all down to my splendid nursing skills,' wailed Debbie, trying hard to look insulted and not succeeding.

Andy said he couldn't care less why Lyall had persuaded her; the important thing was that he had. 'She sits a horse better than any woman I ever knew,' he announced.

But it wasn't Debbie's equestrian skills he valued most; anybody could see that, and when Ellen turned away from Lyall to tease her cousin Lindy whispered as much to him. 'I've never seen such a rapid transfer of affections,' she marvelled.

He looked serious for a moment before saying, 'I have. Of course, this may not lead anywhere, but at the moment it does look as if I'll be losing my housekeeper,' he ended just as Debbie bounced to her feet, saying that if nobody felt like cheese, they might as well go through to the drawing-room and she would bring coffee.

Cups in hand and the mints circulating, talk became general until Ellen, who was on duty, was called to the phone. Returning a few minutes later, she said, 'Sorry to break up the party, folks, but I have to run over to the new estate.' She looked at her cousin. 'Are you all right to walk home, John, or will I drop you off on my way?'

Dr Dunbar thanked her and said he was needing an early night after all the excitement. 'What about you, dear?' he asked his daughter.

'I suppose I may as well,' she began, before being silenced by both Balfours and Andy.

When the two older doctors had gone, she found herself in the kitchen with Lyall. 'OK, where is it?' she asked with mock resignation.

'Last door on the left past the stairs—if you remember,' he said teasingly as he removed his jacket.

'I meant Debbie's plastic apron,' she scolded. 'I suppose we are about to deal with this mess?'

'I am—you're not. Unless you take off that beautiful dress first. Feel free,' he added softly.

Lindy perched on the edge of the table. 'I'm going to enjoy this—watching you work, I mean. It'll make a nice change from scurrying round trying to fulfil your orders.'

'I've changed my mind,' he decided. 'You can fill the dishwasher while I tackle the pans.'

'That's a woman's privilege,' she insisted.

'Washing saucepans? Then please don't let me stop you.'

'Not that! Changing one's mind.'

'And one that some of you exercise far too often,' he retorted thoughtfully.

He can't mean me, so who does he mean? she wondered, as they got to work. They chatted idly for a while until with a muttered exclamation Lyall dropped a large cast-iron pan in the sink. Lindy swung round at the noise. 'What on earth —— ?'

'It's nothing; just this bloody arm.' He retrieved the pot with his left hand and dumped it on the draining-board.

Lindy dashed across to him to look. The flexor muscles of the right wrist were in spasm and must be acutely painful. She seized his arm, ignoring his startled, 'What the hell——?' A deft twist of the wrist and elbow, and seconds later she could feel the spasm subsiding.

'Where the blazes did you pick up that trick?' he asked.

'On a neurology course. It works better on the calf muscles, though.'

'I'm not complaining. Sometimes it sticks like that for as long as twenty minutes.' He hugged her in gratitude. 'What a clever girl you are!'

'Is it still sore?' she asked anxiously.

'A bit—not too much.'

'All the same——' She went over to the freezer and took out a packet of peas to use as an ice pack. 'Here, hold this over the muscle bulk for a bit. It'll deaden the pain and depress the muscle tone.'

'This is the second time you've come to my rescue like this. You're fast becoming indispensable—you know that?' Lyall's voice was caressing.

'Just doing the job I was trained for,' she said unsteadily.

He laid his cheek against hers. 'Is that really all it is? Be honest, now.'

'Well. . .if I was pushed, I guess I'd have to admit I do rather like this particular patient.'

'You're being very circumspect,' he said softly.

'So are you,' she whispered back.

'And yet I think we both know where we're going,' he murmured as Debbie's high heels sounded tap-tap across the hall.

Or rather, I *hope* I know where we're going, Lindy amended silently as they drew apart as Debbie came in. 'You're quite right, darling,' she called back over her shoulder. 'They haven't got very far. We shall have to give them a hand after all.'

Andy would have dropped Lindy off on his way past, but Lyall said firmly that he needed a walk. That provoked a certain amount of teasing from both Andy and Debbie, which Lyall didn't seem to mind any more than Lindy did. Everything's going to be all right now, she told herself as they set off hand in hand.

'Do you really think he and Debbie will make a go of it?' she wondered as Andy's tail-lights disappeared round a bend in the High Street.

'It's a bit soon to tell, but they do seem to agree on fundamentals, and that's the important thing,' answered Lyall.

She was just about to ask what he considered were the fundamentals when she was diverted by the sight of Mrs Turnbull putting out her milk bottles. Quick as thought, she had yanked Lyall into the doorway of the Waverley Café.

'What now?' he wondered, chuckling.

'Ssh!' When she heard a door closing, she peeped out cautiously. 'OK, the coast's clear now. Sorry about that, but we have to be careful,' she offered by way of explanation.

It wasn't enough. 'If you say so, but why?'

'That was Mrs Turnbull putting out those milk bottles.'

'So? Is her name an indication of her nature, then?'

When she stopped giggling, Lindy reminded him that Mrs Turnbull was the town gossip. 'And if she'd seen us walking down the street together at midnight there's no telling what she'd have made of it.'

'So if she happened to see us diving into that doorway like a couple of randy teenagers we can expect her to circulate a real sizzler.'

'She couldn't have, could she? Surely I was too quick for her?'

'Only time will tell,' said Lyall, still laughing. 'But just in case she's watching from the window with her infra-red telescope, let's give her something really interesting to build on.' And with that he bent his head and kissed her fairly thoroughly, after which he put his arm round her waist and kept it there all the way home.

They didn't meet another soul, but putting out the milk bottles was definitely the in thing tonight, because when they turned into the drive of Downside House, there was Lindy's father at it too.

Instinctively they drew back into the dense shadow of the shrubbery. 'If I come any further, and he hears our footsteps——'

'——he'll wait with the door open,' finished Lindy on a whisper. Living at home had distinct disadvantages at times like this.

She was standing with her back to Lyall. Gently he turned her round to face him and kissed her with a hungry desperation. 'We're going to have to get our act together,' he whispered. 'I'm too old for snogging in the shrubbery. I prefer a bit of comfort.'

'As to that, so do I, but you're the one with the flat,' she whispered back.

'And with a sister in it who seems to think she has priority.'

'Nothing to be done there, then.'

'I could wish you sounded a little more disappointed,' he reproached her. 'But I'll think of something, don't you worry. I'm on tomorrow night, but you can practise your driving — if I'm called out.'

'And if you're not? And Debbie's in?'

'Then we'll just have to drive up on the moors. Don't forget the car has a phone.'

'Is that likely, when I got such a rocket for not knowing?' smiled Lindy.

'We've come a long way since then,' he breathed, crushing her close in another fierce embrace.

CHAPTER NINE

'OH, DEBS, you are kind!' exclaimed Lindy one Friday afternoon nearly a month later when Debbie appeared in the treatment-room carrying two steaming mugs of tea.

'Rubbish! This is the third time this week you've failed to show up on time, and as I'm unemployed until Geordie Burns appears for his tetanus injection I thought I'd minister to the busiest member of staff. Any plans for the weekend?'

'I have to go with Pa to see my grandmother on Sunday and I'll be having a driving lesson tomorrow. Why?' asked Lindy.

'Andy says there are masses of blackberries just ripe for picking in that little wood behind their house. I'm organising a picking party for tomorrow afternoon, with dinner cooked by me afterwards, so what about it?'

'I'll have to ask Lyall first. He's wanting to see how I make out in heavy traffic tomorrow.'

'And he tells me that a morning in Hawick should take care of that, so I'll count you both in.' Debbie screwed up her nose. 'But only if you really want to go berry-picking. I'm not allowed to coerce his ewe-lamb.'

Her phrase or his? wondered Lindy. 'Bramble jelly's Pa's favourite,' she said. 'So how can I refuse?'

'I think it's wonderful the way you balance the claims of both men in your life,' admired Debbie. 'If you hadn't taken my darling brother off my hands, I know I'd never have coped.'

'I didn't know I had—taken Lyall off your hands, that is.'

159

'There's no need to be coy with me, dear. He only comes home for bed and breakfast these days. And who was it got whisked off to look over Eildon House when it came on the market? Not me! Very significant, that.'

'That was only because you were so desperate to go to that point-to-point with Andy.'

'Who are you trying to kid, sweetie?' whooped Debbie at her most exuberant.

When she calmed down, Lindy said to her, 'You're supposing a lot more than there is, Debbie. Lyall and I are both quite happy with things as they are.' He seems to be, anyway. . .

'He'd better stop his tricks, then, because the whole town's talking—when they're not speculating about Andy and me, that is. What a terrible place this is for gossip!' sighed Debbie.

'This and every other small town, but I think I hear my wee Fiona pattering down the passage—and you know how it turns your stomach to see her coughing up the way she has to.'

Debbie grimaced. 'I never did get used to that. I could dish out bedpans all day long, but dealing with what comes out the other end—that's quite another ballgame. Why, hello there, young Fi. How's school?'

'So-so, thanks, Nurse. Bobbie Carswell was sick all over my poster today.'

'And you call that so-so? I'd call it diabolical. Well, mustn't hold up the good work. See you.'

'What's diabololical mean, miss?' asked Fiona when Debbie had gone.

'Awful. Dreadful. Very nasty indeed.'

'Poor Bobbie!' sighed Fiona. 'He couldn't help it.'

'I'm sure you're right, Fiona. Now then——'

'I know. Up on the couch and over the pillows on my tummy. I'm warning you, I'm fair bunged up the day,'

Something of an understatement, decided Lindy when Fiona's little chest was clear at last. 'Are you ready, sweetie, or would you like a bit longer to recover?' she asked. Now that Fiona's wee brother Calum was home from the hospital and back on her list, Lindy had got into the habit of pushing Fiona home on her bicycle.

Today, though, they were lucky, because Lyall was free. 'May I have the pleasure of driving you two lovely ladies?' he asked from the doorway of his room as they approached. Fiona's answer was a foregone conclusion, and in no time at all Lyall had dropped them off at the cottage gate. 'See you later,' he whispered to Lindy.

'Why not?' she returned casually for Fiona's benefit.

Fiona was not deceived. 'Can I be your bridesmaid?' she asked as they entered the house.

'What a lovely idea! I'll remember that — if I ever get married,' Lindy answered, sending Fiona off into peals of laughter.

That brought on a tiny frown. Debbie was right when she said that the whole town was talking, but this wasn't the time for bothering about the gossips, when Calum was reluctantly awaiting his treatment.

Afterwards, though, walking home through the autumn dusk, Lindy decided it was time to stop taking each happy day as it came and do some stocktaking.

For the past month, she and Lyall had been virtually inseparable, with the result that just about everybody in Eyretoun — including her father — thought it was only a matter of time until the bells rang out. So why didn't she think so herself? Probably because Lyall had never actually told her he loved her. Was that because he didn't, wasn't sure, or thought it could be taken for granted? He was certainly demonstrative enough — when they were alone. And surely the way he put up with her inept handling of his beautiful car had to count for something?

Lindy was nearly home now, and this period of thought had been no more productive than any previous ones. Phrases like 'only time will tell' and 'wait and see' flitted through her mind. But how much easier it would be to sit it out in the anonymous atmosphere of a city, rather than in this little town where people watched and waited so curiously.

Dr Dunbar and his partner were having tea in the sitting-room when Lindy got back to Downside House. Lyall sent her a caressing look as he got up to pour a cup for her, before answering her father's last remark. 'No, three days should do it, John — and I certainly don't want to be away any longer.' His eyes rested on Lindy as he said that.

Dr Dunbar intercepted that glance, his own expression thoughtful. 'I still think you should take the whole week off. You've not had any holiday all summer, so you must be in need of a break. You could see some shows, go to concerts — look up old friends.'

Lindy asked what they were discussing so earnestly.

'It's a damned nuisance,' said Lyall, 'but I have to go to London for a few days to deal with problems arising out of my grandfather's will — and your father is trying to persuade me to make a holiday of it.'

'It's not a bad idea — the holiday, I mean,' she considered. 'You should have a break before the winter. We'll be even busier then.' And if you miss me enough, then perhaps when you come back. . .

'Are you trying to get rid of me?' Lyall asked plaintively.

'However did you guess?' she asked teasingly. She always tried to keep things light when her father was there. 'And while we're on the subject of holidays, is it all right with you two if I take my usual two weeks next February to go skiing with the Edinburgh crowd?'

'Of course, dear,' returned her father, while Lyall said he'd like to know a bit more about this Edinburgh crowd.

That night, Dr Dunbar failed to exercise his usual tact, going neither to his study nor to the golf club after supper. Lindy wondered why. So did Lyall. When she went to see him off as usual he said, 'It's not like your father to play the chaperon, is it, darling?'

'It's a bit hard if a man can't sit by his own fireside sometimes,' she replied.

'True, but if we'd known he'd be here all the time, we could have gone to the flat. Debs is out somewhere with Andy. Never mind, we'll be at the flat tomorrow night.' He took her in his arms and kissed her lingeringly before asking, 'This skiing crowd. Is it mixed?'

'Very. Folk from all walks of life.'

He shook her gently by the shoulders. 'That's not what I meant, and you know it.'

'All right then, yes. Boys and girls both. Satisfied?'

'No.' His voice dropped to a whisper. 'But who knows? By then you may not want to go. I'll pick you up early tomorrow morning, my love. Hawick's worse than the West End on Saturdays, and you need the practice.'

Next morning Lindy was ready and waiting. Eagerly. Last night Lyall had called her his love, and he'd never done that before. A quick hug, a kiss and he said, 'you look quite gorgeous today. Green is definitely your colour.'

'Green for envy,' she said.

'You need envy no one when you can look as you do,' he assured her.

And neither I do when you look at me like that, she thought. Only——

'Ready, my angel?'

'As I'll ever be. . .'

They set off. 'Are you sure this is the best road to

Hawick, Lyall?' asked Lindy a while later, the second time they met the 'Bends for Two Miles' sign.

'For you, my sweet one, yes. It's good practice in matching speed with the correct gear. Not to mention steering practice.'

'You've always got an answer.'

'I don't know about that. You've left me speechless more than once.'

'Could do better if she tried, then. Oh look, Lyall — a red squirrel!'

'Keep your eyes on the road and never mind the wildlife unless it's in your path,' he ordered.

'You're a brute!'

'And you're delicious — most of the time. Why are you stopping?'

'Because I think you deserve a kiss for that, and I'm not yet skilful enough to drive at the same time. There! Was that not nice?'

'Lovely — now off you go. A bend on a tree-lined road isn't the best place for this sort of thing.' A loud blast from a following bus underlined that, and Lindy promised to behave in future — at least while the car was on the move.

She certainly needed all her concentration when they reached the congested streets of the busy town. 'Why did that nasty man shout at me like that?' she wondered after half an hour of stress spent with her teeth tightly clenched.

'I expect it was because you went the wrong side of that traffic island, dear.'

'So did the car in front.'

'Two wrongs don't make a right. Take the next left,' instructed Lyall.

'No! I am not going round that horrible double roundabout a second time.'

'You'll make a much better job of it next time.'

'Oh, all right, then.' A few minutes later Lindy said triumphantly, 'That wasn't very bright of you, was it? Now we're in a dead end.'

'A splendid opportunity to practise your three-point turn.'

'I hate you!'

'You'll get over it,' he predicted confidently.

Lindy slumped in her seat. 'I am now a complete and utter wreck,' she announced tragically.

After one look at her tight little face he said gently, 'Lindy, I'm so sorry—I should have realised I was pushing you too hard, but you were doing so well. Shall we swap over?'

'If you don't mind.'

They headed back towards Eyretoun and soon Lyall stopped the car beside a neat little wayside inn. I couldn't eat a thing,' she protested, but she changed her mind when she saw the tempting array of salads.

'Feeling better now?' Lyall asked as they set off again.

'Much better, thank you. And that road coming up on the left will take us straight to the farm.'

'I'll remember that, but today I have to go back to the flat first. I'm expecting rather an important letter.'

'How exciting! I don't think I've ever had an important letter.'

'You will, little one, if you ever fall into the hands of solicitors,' he promised.

Lindy stayed in the car while Lyall went looking for his letter. When ten minutes had passed and he hadn't come back, she went to look for him. A short passage led to the stairs up to the flat, and that was where she found him. He was leaning against the wall, staring at nothing. He looked dazed. In the hand dangling at his side, he held a single sheet of paper.

His shock was contagious, yet inhibiting, freezing Lindy in dread on the doorstep, even though she longed to rush forward and comfort him. A little cough to ease the constriction in her throat sounded like a pistol shot in the tense hush. 'You — you got it, then?'

He stirred and looked towards her, unseeing. 'What?'

'Your important letter. It's come.'

He focused on her with a visible effort, dredging up a twisted smile. 'Oh, that. Yes — it's come.'

'And it was bad news.' How could she doubt that?

It seemed an age before he said reluctantly, 'That — depends.' A tense pause. 'But it'll all be — be sorted out when I get to London.'

'That's good. I don't like to see you so distressed.'

He reached out as though to touch her, then let his arm fall back to his side. 'What a dear, loyal little soul you are! I wish to God I'd ——' He stopped abruptly, leaving her desperate to know what it was he'd so nearly said. Her sixth sense was telling her it would have been very revealing.

'Lyall — don't you ——?' she began.

'Yes, you're right. Debbie will be wondering what's become of us.' He straightened up and stuffed the letter into the inside pocket of his jacket. 'Do you want to drive, or have you had enough for one day?'

'I certainly have,' Lindy said quietly. Enough of driving, and more than enough of evasion. . . How could she concentrate enough to drive or do anything else when she was bursting to know what had upset him so much? And he had made it so very clear that he wasn't telling?

He looked up at the sky which was now grey and cloudy. 'We must call at the house and get you a thicker sweater. It could be chilly up on the hill now that the sun's gone.'

'I'll pick up a waterproof as well.' He's as far away from me now as he's ever been, she realised with anguish.

'Good thinking,' he returned stiltedly, adding, 'Oh, good morning, Mrs Turnbull,' as that lady plodded laboriously past, leaning on two sticks. 'I thought we'd agreed she didn't need sticks any more, Lindy,' he said as they got into the car.

'We did. But she likes the sympathy they get her.'

'Straight to the point as always,' he observed more easily as they moved off. He wasn't himself, though. That letter had come between them in some strange way that Lindy couldn't understand.

As agreed, they stopped at Downside House before going on to the Robertson farm. Lyall passed remarks and Lindy answered. On the surface, all was well. But he didn't comment on her quiet abstraction as he would certainly have done earlier. Before he had read that letter. But he had said it would all be sorted out once he got to London. She must try to be satisfied with that.

Lindy was wondering if Debbie would notice the change in her brother's manner, knowing she'd be sure to comment if she did. She was to be disappointed. Debbie was much too interested in everything Andy said and did, and Lyall himself seemed cheerful enough now; enough to deceive anybody who hadn't seen his stricken look after reading that letter. He was so cheerful in fact that as the afternoon wore on, Lindy began to wonder if she had overestimated its effect. Or was that just because that was what she wanted to believe?

'What's the matter with you?' asked Debbie at that point as she peered through a gap in the hedge. 'You've been standing there staring into space for the past five minutes. I know you're in love, dear, but aren't we all? So get picking!'

'I was miles away,' Lindy said, glancing round to make sure Lyall hadn't heard. And yet Debbie's blithe confidence was reassuring. Who better placed than she to know her brother's feelings? Lindy stopped wondering and got picking as directed.

The rain that had been threatening all afternoon soon began to fall, but by then the baskets were filled and they hurried back to the house.

'Twenty-three pounds plus! Who'd have thought it?' Debbie asked gleefully when the crop had been weighed and divided out to everybody's satisfaction. 'That was a good day's work.'

'But it's not over yet, my love,' Andy reminded her. 'Don't forget you promised us dinner.'

'Then somebody not five feet from here had better stop lounging and drive me home,' his love told him smartly.

'Y'know, this is a very good idea,' said Andy to Lindy some time later, when they were all in the kitchen at the flat helping Debbie to put the finishing touches to the meal. 'Debs and I are running out of places where we can go without getting nudge, nudge, wink, wink, to put us off our food. You and Lyall must be finding that too.'

'Just what he was saying only this morning at break-fast,' the irrepressible Debbie butted in. 'That's why we're all slaving away here. Lyall, must you make such a mess with that cream?'

'Sorry, Debs — the bowl slipped. I'll clean it up.'

'That you will, my lad. I'm nobody's slave. Andy, my darling, please note.'

'I'm noting, but can we eat now, please? I'm starving!'

'When are you not?' asked Debbie, kissing him lingeringly.

Happy as can be, the lucky things, thought Lindy. She had seen Lyall's expression when Debbie said what she did about his breakfast speech, and she knew very well why the bowl had slipped. Since that carefree remark, he had received a letter — a letter which somehow had altered everything.

Yet by the time they'd polished off soup, navarin of lamb and a large bramble tart, Lyall was almost as cheerful as his sister and Andy. Lindy began to relax herself. When Debbie went to make coffee, the others wandered through to the sitting-room. 'So how long will you be away?' Andy asked Lyall.

'I should be able to get the sleeper up on Friday.'

'I thought Debbie said you were only going for three days,' returned Andy, voicing Lindy's thoughts.

'That was the original idea, but things are proving more complicated than I expected.'

'These things always do,' said Andy. 'My grandfather had been dead for more than three years before everything was settled.'

'That's very encouraging,' Lyall was saying when Debbie came in.

'What is?' she enquired curiously.

'Andy was just saying it took more than three years to settle his grandfather's estate.'

'And I thought Scots law was supposed to be so much less complicated than English. Which reminds me — what did old Scantlebury have to say, Lyall?'

'About what?'

'So it didn't arrive after all, then — God bless our Royal Mail! Lyall was expecting a letter from our lawyer today,' Debbie explained. 'Hi, where are you off to?' she demanded as Lyall made for the door. 'I have remembered the sugar—for once.'

'But I forgot about Scantlebury's letter, would you believe?'

'So it did come—but you can't remember what he said. And you're supposed to be so bright!'

'The fact is, I haven't——' He stopped, sending Lindy an anxious glance. 'You'd better read it yourself,' he ended lamely, going out and shutting the door.

'And he used to be so methodical and down to earth,' sighed his sister. 'No need to look far for the cause of this witlessness, though,' she added with an impish look for Lindy.

But Lindy was staring down into the High Street from her station by the window, and remembering something she'd discounted in her anxiety at Lyall's obvious distress that morning. The sheet of paper he'd been holding had been of thick, creamy vellum as well as smaller in size than was commonly used for business letters. So the letter that had caused him such disquiet was not from the lawyer at all, because as surely as if he'd admitted it, Lindy knew he hadn't even opened that one yet. So what was this other serious problem that was to be solved during his visit to London?

Lyall came back and handed the lawyer's letter to his sister. 'As you'll see, things are a bit complicated,' he told her.

Debbie read the letter and handed it back to him, looking surprised. 'I have to say it seems straightforward enough to me, but then I've no head for business. Now then, does everyone want their coffee black?'

Lindy sat down heavily on the window seat. Lyall had taken a chance by saying things were a bit complicated. He wanted her to go on believing his only problems were legal ones, but Debbie—not in the know—hadn't backed him up. So this other problem. Was it something that she wouldn't approve of, or might be hurt by? Oh, what could it be?

Lyall had come over to close the curtains. 'Come and sit by the fire,' he said gently, taking Lindy's hand and pulling her to her feet.

'I hadn't noticed it was lit,' she said tonelessly.

'And guess who'll have to clear out the fireplace in the morning,' invited Debbie good-humouredly from her seat on the sofa, cuddled up to Andy. 'That's yours, Lindy — the one with the cream.'

'Thanks.'

'Are you feeling all right, dear?' asked Debbie. 'You're very quiet tonight.'

'I'm fine,' Lindy insisted. 'Well, a bit tired perhaps. . .' Funny how we all make that excuse when we don't want folk to know we're troubled, she thought.

'It's my fault, said Lyall, startling her. 'I gave her too tough a time in Hawick this morning.'

'So when is your test, Lindy?' asked Andy.

'In about three weeks.'

'You'll pass and no trouble,' he predicted. 'But I remember when Mum first started. . .' He launched into a long story about his mother's early motoring experiences which, as well as being amusing, spared the others the trouble of talking. When it ended, Lyall said he thought he ought to take Lindy home as she had to be up early next morning for her trip to Perth. He was looking gloomy again now, so Lindy told him not to bother; she would walk. 'You don't really think I'd let you do that, do you?' he asked quietly.

'But — all that mess in the kitchen to be dealt with. . .' The truth was, she was dreading being alone with him. Afraid that he wouldn't confide in her and fearful of what she'd hear if he did. Am I getting neurotic? she wondered as Lyall retorted firmly that it wasn't their turn for kitchen duty.

'I wonder what's gone wrong there?' she heard Andy say as the door closed behind them.

'So do I,' she whispered, but Lyall was fetching her anorak, so it was easy for him to pretend he hadn't heard, though she was convinced he had.

'It's quite a while since you went to see your grandmother,' he observed as they set off.

'She's been away. In fact, she's hardly ever at home.'

'She's obviously fit, then.'

'Amazingly so — for eighty-two,' said Lindy.

'A good example for the Mrs Turnbulls of this world.'

'Yes — splendid.' They'd soon be home and she hadn't managed to get the conversation round to the only thing that mattered. She'd thought she couldn't bear to know what was souring their relationship, but anything was better than this torturing uncertainty. On the doorstep, she cut through more pleasantries to say urgently, 'Something is very wrong, Lyall — I know it! Can't you tell me what it is?'

He took so long to answer that she began to think he wouldn't. Then at last he said heavily, 'I think I told you this morning that it would all be settled by the time I got back from London. And it will. We'll talk about it then, but in the meantime — please trust me. The last thing I want is for you to be — involved. . .' His voice trailed painfully away.

'Then just ——'

'No, Lindy I can't! Not now. It would only make things worse.' He silenced her with a sudden, desperate embrace. Then, after kissing her once with the same angry desperation, he got back into the car and drove off at speed.

CHAPTER TEN

'WHAT a pity we didn't think of asking Lyall to leave the L-plates,' observed Dr Dunbar as they set off next morning. 'You could have got in some useful practice today, dear.'

'I did think of it,' Lindy answered. 'Then something drove the idea right out of my head.' The something being that damned letter. 'Just as well, really. The strain might have been too much for you.'

'You really must get out of this habit of putting yourself down, Lindy,' urged her father. 'Lyall says you're shaping up very well.'

'That's very kind of him.' She changed the subject to another, less upsetting. 'I wonder how we'll find Gran today?'

Her father sent her a narrowed glance before answering. Did he suspect that all was not well? 'Much as usual, I expect,' he said at last. 'Complaining bitterly that she can't get about as she used to one minute, then outlining her next trip abroad the next.'

Today, though, Gran had something else besides foreign travel on her mind. She ran true to form during lunch at a nearby hotel — they always took her out to save her cooking — and as always, Lindy went to the kitchen to make coffee when they returned to the flat. But when she carried the tray into the living-room, her father and Gran were talking about Lindy's cousin Clare.

'I blame her parents,' Gran was saying. 'They should never have let her marry him in the first place.'

Her son said it was easy enough to be wise after the

event, and anyway, how much say did parents have
these days?

Gran brushed that aside with one of her grand ges-
tures. 'Anybody with half an eye could see what would
happen. Craig doted—simply doted—on Tina Fraser
and he only married Clare after Tina married that
foreigner. But he soon ran off with somebody else, so
home comes Tina in floods of tears to reclaim her faithful
poodle, who can't set up house with her fast enough,
leaving Clare holding the baby. Literally! Did I tell you
she's pregnant? What a mess!'

'Nobody could have foreseen that turn of events,'
maintained Dr Dunbar.

Gran snorted at such naïveté. 'When a man is as
hooked on a woman as Craig is on Tina, there's no cure
for it—none! Clare hadn't a hope. I begged her not to
marry him, but she wouldn't listen. Told me it was all
over between Craig and Tina.' Gran snorted. 'That sort
of obsession never is—never! Lindy dear, why are you
looking like that? You never liked Craig much either, as
I recall.'

'I'm shocked, Granny.' And not only for poor Clare. . .
Lindy scarcely heard the rest of the conversation, and as
soon as the coffee was finished she gathered the cups and
whisked them off to the kitchen, where she took her time
about washing up.

This is all nonsense, Lindy told herself. There's no
parallel. Just because Lyall wouldn't tell me what was
troubling him, it doesn't follow that he's another Craig,
obsessed with a woman who's come back into his life.
And yet there *is* something—I know there is. What more
likely than another woman—one from whom he's never
quite broken free? Who wrote that letter. . . So many
pointers! His holding back. Would he ever have thawed
but for Michael? And he's never said he loves me. It's a

though I'm a—a substitute. Second-best. And what about that remark of Debbie's after she met Elspeth? 'I'd have thought he'd had enough of her sort!'

Lindy swayed and gripped the edge of the sink for support. She must stop this, or she'd go mad. And yet there *was* something. . .

Be practical. Be positive. Could she get Pa to leave in time for her to see Lyall before he left to catch the night train? A whole week of this uncertainty and she really would go mad!

More than once on the homeward journey, Lindy felt her father glancing her way thoughtfully. He spoke out at last. 'You're very quiet, dear.'

'I can't get my mind off poor Clare, Pa.' And not only off Clare. . .

'That's a bad business right enough. I'd like to horsewhip that spineless husband of hers!' burst out the good man with uncharacteristic heat.

'That wouldn't do any good, Pa. As Gran says, when a man is that dotty about a woman, there's nothing to be done. What time do you think we'll get home?'

'About eight, I should think—unless there's a hold-up at the Forth Bridge. Why?'

'Oh, I just thought I might call round and see Elspeth. I've not seen her for ages.'

Her father gave her another of those questioning looks, but all he said was, 'I'll drop you off then, if you like.'

'Yes—please, Pa.'

The minute her father's car turned the corner after dropping her off at the mill, Lindy set off in the opposite direction, towards the High Street and Lyall's flat. The Ferrari stood ready at the kerb, but there was no sign of Andy's Jaguar, so the chances were that Debbie was out and Lyall was alone. Ring the doorbell quickly before your courage fails!

Lyall came to the door, looking remote and unfamiliar in a town suit. When he saw Lindy, he gasped audibly. 'Lindy! I didn't expect. . .' His voice trailed away.

'I can believe that,' she retorted, pressing home her advantage, even though her knees felt they would give way at any minute. 'Are you going to let me in or not?'

'Yes — of course.' He stood aside and in the harsh light of the vestibule she could see how troubled he was. Dark shadows under his eyes showed that he hadn't slept the previous night any better than she had. A quick stab of pity gave way to satisfaction. So he did have some conscience—— 'I was just on the point of leaving,' he said awkwardly.

Lindy mustered all her courage. 'It won't do! You can't fob me off with half truths. There's — there's somebody else, isn't there? And you're going to see her!'

'Who told you that?' he asked grimly.

'Nobody. But I'm not totally daft. That letter — she wrote it. And now I suppose you're going to take her back!'

That struck home, and Lyall winced visibly. 'You see everything in black and white, but it's not that simple,' he said heavily. 'Sylvia and I were together a long time and I — loved her very much. But she left me. And then I came here and met you.' His face softened, almost to tenderness. 'You were like a breath of pure, clean air — and very appealing. But I wasn't free of — her, and didn't want to hurt you. That's why I hung back at first. And why I didn't tell you about her when we did eventually. . .because then it seemed unnecessary. The past was — past.'

'But it wasn't, was it? She's resurfaced. And now you're going to see her.' It was a statement, not question.

'I have to. How else can I ever —— ?'

'Oh, don't pretend there's any doubt,' Lindy broke in desperately. 'We both know you're going to take her back! If you weren't, you'd have said so. And if I were the dim little doormat you think I am, I'd probably tell you how glad I was to be here to provide the temporary comfort. Well, I'm not! I'm furious! You've made me a laughing stock in this town. Why the hell couldn't you have left me alone?' She wheeled round and wrenched open the door, running out into the road.

A second later Lyall followed, but Lindy knew the town much better than he did, and by the time he reached the pavement, she was out of sight. She listened to him pounding up the street and back, and not until she heard him drive away did she emerge from her hiding place. Then as an added precaution, she went home by a very roundabout route.

She hadn't expected to see Lyall's car crossing the green. He must have called at the house, and what would Pa have made of that? She walked round a bit longer, trying to think what to say.

'Lyall looked in on his way to Berwick,' said Dr Dunbar when Lindy opened the sitting-room door. 'I told him you were at Elspeth's, but he didn't seem very keen on going there. He waited as long as he dared without risk of missing his train.'

'Never mind,' she managed mildly. 'I did wish him a happy holiday — last night.' She went up to her father and kissed his lined cheek. 'I'm packing you off to bed now,' she said tenderly. 'You've got a busy week ahead, m'lad.'

I managed that well, she thought, but her protective shield buckled once she shut her bedroom door. She lay on her bed, dry-eyed and utterly miserable, until the blessed relief of tears. Then she cried herself into the sleep of utter exhaustion.

* * *

'I'll not be in to lunch today, dear,' her father said to Lindy at breakfast next morning. 'One of the drug companies is hosting a lunch for Border GPs at the Eyretoun Arms.'

'Lucky old you, Pa. I hope they give you smoked salmon,' she joked as she got up to fetch the toast. I'll ask Debbie to lunch, she thought. The sooner I start laying false trails, the better. . .

The morning dragged by, and an unscheduled fact-finding visit from Mrs Turnbull did nothing to cheer. 'You said to come in any time the rubbers my sticks wore out,' she reminded Lindy.

'But you don't really need sticks now, do you?'

'Not according to Dr Balfour and that bossy wee surgeon at the hospital, but they haven't got my feet.' Mrs Turnbull took a deep breath and got down to business. 'I'm surprised you're not away to London with Dr Balfour, dear. It would have been a nice change for you — and you could have bought your wedding dress!'

You old cow, thought Lindy, uncharacteristically spiteful in her hurt. 'When it's time to get my outfit for her wedding, I'm sure Nurse Balfour will tell me,' she returned, thankful to have turned aside the dart, yet feeling guilty at having sacrificed Debbie on the altar of necessity. 'There! I've fitted new ferrules to your sticks but those are the last you're getting. I happen to agree with the doctors. And now you'll have to excuse me — I'm extremely busy today.'

So Mrs Turnbull departed, thwarted for the moment but it couldn't be long before she and all the town knew that the doctor's daughter had been jilted. Not in fact — Lyall hadn't proposed — but fact had never bothered scandalmongers yet!

Debbie had also had a bad morning, and she went on about it for so long over lunch that Lindy, in her essimism, felt sure Debbie guessed why she'd been sked and was trying to stop Lindy getting in a word. 'It ounds as if you're almost sorry you came to Eyretoun,' he said, when Debbie eventually ran out of breath.

That made Debbie giggle. 'Dear me, I must have been verdoing the aggro if you can think that! No, Lindy, oming to Eyretoun is the best thing I've ever done.' A ender smile suffused her face, leaving Lindy in no doubt vhere her thoughts were now.

'I doubt if your brother would say the same. He's got uite a problem now, hasn't he?'

'You mean when Andy and I get married and he's left o look after himself.' Debbie had misunderstood, and lmost certainly on purpose.

'That's not what I mean at all, Debbie. I meant that oming to Eyretoun was hardly the best thing he ever lid. Sylvia's not likely to settle down here, is she? I'll bet he's the sort who likes the bright lights.'

Debbie stared at Lindy across the table, and Lindy tared as steadily back. 'I — I don't know what to say,' Debbie breathed at last. 'That is, I don't know what ou're talking about.'

'You mean you didn't know that Lyall has gone to London as much to see her as to see your family lawyer?'

'B-but. . .he said he wasn't going to tell you. He said here was no point in upsetting you — unnecessarily.' Debbie was really distressed now. 'Look, Lindy — I'm ot speaking for Lyall, but this is how I see it. He really s genuinely fond of you, and if Sylvia hadn't eappeared — which nobody could have expected — then 'm sure. . .' She stopped, unsure how to proceed. 'But hey were together such a long time, and he doted on er.' That word again — the word Gran had used about Clare's erring husband. 'And that letter completely nocked him for six. You can see his dilemma?'

'Oh, yes,' said Lindy. 'As I said at the start of this conversation, coming to Eyretoun was hardly the best thing he ever did. Still, he'll sort it all out. He's very resourceful.' Then she picked up her spoon and started on her soup. 'Eat up, Debbie, it's getting cold.'

'I'm not hungry!' wailed Debbie, getting to her feet and running round the table to embrace Lindy. 'You're such a darling! I'd really hoped. . . God, I could kill that bloody woman!' she exclaimed, bursting into tears and running out of the kitchen.

Lindy would have liked a good cry herself, but she couldn't indulge. Starting the afternoon sessions with red-rimmed eyes was no way to keep everybody guessing.

As if she hadn't enough to put up with that day, Lindy had to meet Elspeth of all people, on her way home from treating Calum Duffus. They'd hardly seen one another since Andy took up with Debbie. 'Long time, no see,' said Elspeth.

'Yes, isn't it amazing — in a small place like this?'

'The town grapevine has kept me informed of your progress, though,' Elspeth returned spitefully.

'Naturally. It thrives on gossip. Has it told you that Lyall thinks I'll soon be ready to take my driving test?'

'Are you asking me to believe that car driving is all he's been teaching you?'

'Of course. Because it's true. Did he never tell you about Sylvia, then? Obviously not,' Lindy rushed on when Elspeth looked blank. 'Keep this under your hat,' she breathed, knowing fine that Elspeth wouldn't, 'but they're probably getting together again. And am I glad I got my driving lessons first! Sylvia sounds the jealous type. Must dash now. Pa will be looking for his supper.'

By then Lindy was almost in tears, but at least that was another smoke-screen laid. What was really needed was to be seen about with another man. What a pity Bi had recently taken up with his partner's daughter. And yet was it? Having been used herself, Lindy knew how painful that was. Besides, using people for your own ends was immoral.

'There was a phone call for you, just after you set off with young Fiona,' said Dr Dunbar when Lindy reached home. 'Mrs Gavin took the message; I've got it here somewhere.' He rummaged in his pocket and pulled out a crumpled scrap of paper.

It was Jeannie who'd rung, and she wanted Lindy to ring up her boyfriend Gordon at the District Hospital. How very intriguing! As soon as the vegetables were on, Lindy dialled the number.

Gordon had been seconded for six months and was feeling lonely, so would Lindy like to meet him for a jar and a natter tomorrow night? Since it was his girlfriend who'd suggested it, meeting Gordon would hardly be making use of him, so Lindy asked why not, and they settled on a pub in Melrose, which would be halfway for both of them. She'd have preferred it if he'd come to Eyretoun. They would have been seen together then and a rumour might have gone round about Lindy Dunbar's new boyfriend. But Gordon didn't have a car either, so Melrose made more sense.

As it turned out, the meeting wasn't entirely unfruitful. When Lindy went to collect her case-notes the morning after, Mrs Gavin asked Lindy if she'd got her message. Lindy said yes, thanks, and as a result she had got in touch with her old friend Gordon.

'And who's Gordon?' asked Debbie, who also happened to be collecting her morning list.

'Another of my Edinburgh friends who's just started an SHO job over at the hospital.'

'That's nice,' returned Debbie, looking as if she couldn't decide whether she meant that or not. She followed Lindy down the corridor. 'Listen, love — I got a bit emotional over lunch on Monday, and I want to apologise. I took a very gloomy view of things — and I'm sorry about that too. I'm sure everything will turn out for the best.'

'Things usually do, don't they?' returned Lindy, sounding brighter than she felt. 'Only it's not always apparent at the time. How's Andy?'

'Fine. Look, why don't you come round to the flat and have supper with us tomorrow night?'

'Thanks, Debs, but I'm going out with Gordon again.'

'Oh, that's all right, then. Just so long as — as. . .' Poor Debbie floundered to a full stop, torn between her liking for Lindy and her loyalty to her brother, who might or might not be in the process of making the wrong decision, down there in London.

Lindy understood as clearly as if Debbie had spelt it out. 'I do like you, Debbie,' she said impulsively. 'I hope we'll always be friends.'

'Nurse Balfour!' That was Ellen calling.

'Coming, Doctor,' Debbie called back, but first she rushed at Lindy and gave her a quick hug. 'Lyall's right about you,' she said. 'You're pure gold all through.'

Lindy supposed that was nice to know, even if he did prefer his women to be made of dross. It meant he would see her go out of his life with some regret. But nothing like the pain she felt at having been so stupid as to fall in love with him.

'Sorry to have kept you waiting, Mr Bain,' she apologised.

'That's all right, m'lass. What's a minute or two when it would have taken me all morning to get to the hospital and back for my treatment if your father hadn't built this fine new clinic?'

So the townsfolk were giving her father all the credit.

Good! Now it wouldn't look so odd when Lyall left Eyretoun, as Sylvia would surely make him do. By now, they'd probably selected a suite of rooms in Harley Street. A private GP didn't carry quite the cachet of a Society surgeon, but these last months without him had obviously taught Sylvia to count her blessings. Oh, Clare! What's the matter with us that we should both be such losers? thought Lindy.

'Ready when you are, Miss Dunbar.'

'Coming, Mr Bain. Oh, splendid! I can tell by the nimble way you climbed up on the couch that your back is less painful today. So after the deep heat, I shall give you some strengthening exercises. Staying in bed as long as you did before calling the doctor has made you very unfit.' Lindy's tone was bright, belying her inner sadness, but then one must always be cheerful for the patients.

Wednesday dragged slowly by. Only Fiona to come now and then Calum to be visited at home. There would be another difficult evening of making sure that Pa didn't get an inkling of her misery and then another dreary day tomorrow. Later, though, some of the towns-folk would be sure to spot her at the Eyretoun Arms with Gordon. And she meant to look as if she was having the time of her life.

Next morning, Lindy opened the connecting door between dining-room and surgery, then stopped dead at the sight of Lyall disappearing down the new corridor. He'd come back a day early. Why? Quietly she shut the door again. Had he sent Sylvia packing, or did he want to get the inevitable unpleasantness over as soon as possible? It wasn't difficult to choose. Thank heavens she'd spotted him; now she'd not be making a spectacle of herself when they met. A few minutes to rev up her courage and Lindy opened the door again, but when she crossed the waiting-room, there was no sign of Lyall.

'Dr Balfour's back early,' announced Mrs Gavin as Lindy collected her records. 'He offered to do your father's surgery, but Doctor wouldn't let him. So he's taken all the visits.'

'How very thoughtful,' responded Lindy brightly, and feeling quite proud of herself. 'Especially after a night in the train. And here am I late on parade! What a good thing he's gone out, or I might have got a rocket.'

She left Mrs Gavin staring after her in puzzlement. In common with the rest of the townsfolk, she thought that Dr Balfour was head over heels about his partner's daughter.

All morning Lindy was on edge, listening for Lyall's familiar step, and between patients she rehearsed some light, sophisticated comments. She didn't see him until lunchtime, though, when he was talking to one of the community nurses in the waiting-room. 'Excuse me,' he said abruptly as Lindy approached.

She'd been practising her smile for hours. 'Good morning, Doctor—nice to see you back. I hope you enjoyed the break,' she got out, not slowing down at all and marching on into the house, where she shut and locked the door. But she was trembling violently and her legs felt like jelly.

She tottered across to the sideboard and poured herself a brandy. If Pa smelt that on her breath, he'd think she'd gone mad, but this was an emergency. Suck a Polo, then—and bless Mr Bain, who brought her a packet every time he came for treatment.

Somebody tried the connecting door, then hammered on it. 'Lindy! It's me—Lyall!'

She froze in silence. The knocking was not repeated and she could hear his steps receding on the tiled floor of the passage. Perversely, she was sorry now that their meeting was postponed. It had to come, so it would have been better to get it over.

She heard the front door open and close and realised her father was home before she'd done anything about lunch. Hurry to the kitchen and cobble something together. She opened the door into the hall and came face to face with Lyall.

In contrast to her inner turmoil, he seemed confident, almost carefree. How unfair — and infuriating! 'We have to talk,' he said firmly.

'Not now. I don't have time to listen.'

'You must, Lindy!'

'Must? *Must*?' she echoed. 'What's this, then? You wouldn't talk to me when I wanted you to, and there was only one conclusion to be drawn from that — and I drew it! And you didn't tell me I was wrong, so — '

'Because in all honesty, I couldn't. Then.'

'Because you weren't sure, you'll say.'

'Exactly! You *do* understand!'

'Oh, yes, I understand. I understand that I offered you friendship — friendship you abused. You let me think you were growing fond of me. But the minute you heard from that — from *her*, I counted for nothing!'

'That's not true,' Lyall broke in angrily.

'It is — it is! And now you say you want to talk. As if there was anything left to say. Well, I've got something to say,' Lindy hurtled on, unconscious of any irony. 'I could forgive you for making me a laughing stock in this town, but never — *never* will I forgive you for what you're doing to my father and Ellen. Letting them in for all that expense and upheaval and then walking out — '

'Shut up!' he bellowed, taking her by the shoulders and shaking her roughly. 'Shut up — and listen!'

Dr Dunbar came in just in time to hear that. He crept by unnoticed and shut himself in the kitchen.

Lindy shook herself free. 'Typical male!' she taunted. 'Resort to violence when you've got no case!'

'No case!' Lyall thundered, thrusting her into the dining-room and kicking the door shut. He pushed her into a chair and, grasping the arms, he bent down and glared her into a quivering silence. 'If you so much as utter one sound before I've finished, I'll not be answerable for the consequences!' he hissed through clenched teeth.

Lindy stared up at him, mesmerised. After a long tense moment, Lyall slowly straightened up. But now that he had silenced her, he seemed to have difficulty finding the words he wanted. The silence was almost too painful to be borne. Tension mounted, and just as Lindy felt she'd scream if it went on a moment longer, Lyall said abruptly, 'I'd better start at the beginning. Sylvia is a model, a very successful one.' The woman in the newspaper, realised Lindy. 'I was still a student when we met, and we lived together for nine years. She liked the idea of my being a surgeon, and when I — told her I had to change course, she flew into a temper, insisting that it wasn't necessary because my hand was improving and I was only doing it to punish her for letting that door swing back. I tried to explain the difference between gross functional recovery and the sort of fine precision control a surgeon needs, but she couldn't or wouldn' take it in. She threatened to leave, and although the relationship had been deteriorating for some time, I stil felt — when she did walk out — that I could never be happy again. All I wanted then was to get right away and bury myself in my work.

'Eyretoun seemed the perfect place. Plenty of work, complete change of scene and with nothing but happ associations.' He looked at Lindy then for the first time since he'd started speaking. His expression was tender. 'I found you and gradually came to life again.

'Then Sylvia wrote, saying she was sorry and wanted to come back to me. I was in turmoil; beset by memories of our good times, unable to reject her out of hand, despising myself for such weakness—and all the time worrying about you. I'd become so fond of you, but in so short a time. I had to wonder if it might be just a rebound reaction, when Sylvia could still—disturb me so much. I couldn't tell you about her letter! I didn't know what the hell I was feeling, but I did know I couldn't bear to hurt you.

'I met her as she asked,' he went on. 'She was even more beautiful than I remembered, but a strange thing was happening. For the first time ever, I was seeing how selfish and scheming and mercenary she was. She had heard about the money, of course. I was still conscious of her appeal, but I didn't want her any more. I was free—and it was a glorious feeling.'

'I see,' Lindy breathed slowly, still bemused.

'Oh, Lindy, I wonder if you do? Don't you understand? It was getting to know you that had opened my eyes. No man who'd been blessed with your love could possibly be taken in by somebody like her.'

'Here, hold on a minute,' she protested. 'I don't remember telling you I love you.'

'Don't you?' he queried.

'Do you love me?'

He clenched his fists in frustration. 'What the blazes do you think I've been saying for the last five minutes?'

'Quite a lot—and very well put, most of it—but I didn't hear you say you loved me.'

He pulled her to her feet and snatched her close, his eyes blazing down into hers. 'Well, I do! I love you. I adore you. And if you won't have me, I won't be answerable for the consequences.'

'You're repeating yourself. That's what you said when I wouldn't shut up a while back.'

A painful spasm contorted his face. 'You're torment-ing me,' he groaned. 'I know I deserve it, but darling — please. . .'

'Oh, Lyall!' Lindy surrendered her mouth to his, and with it all her devotion.

'What a celebration we'll have tonight!' he exulted some time later.

Lindy caught her breath. 'Oh, dear — poor Gordon. . .'

He tightened his hold on her. 'Gordon? Who's Gordon?'

'A friend. A doctor who's just transferred to the Roxburgh. We have a date tonight.'

'And I had practically to snatch you out of the arms of the local vet! Just how many men have you got dangling after you, my girl?'

'Quality is always in great demand,' she told him provocatively.

'Are you threatening me?' he demanded.

'No — just trying to make sure that you appreciate me.'

'I do — and I always will, my darling,' Lyall breathed fervently, gathering her close again and kissing her fit to melt her very bones.

— MEDICAL ♥ ROMANCE —

The books for enjoyment this month are:

A BORDER PRACTICE Drusilla Douglas
A SONG FOR DR ROSE Margaret Holt
THE LAST EDEN Marion Lennox
HANDFUL OF DREAMS Margaret O'Neill

♥   ♥   ♥   ♥   ♥

Treats in store!

Watch next month for the following absorbing stories:

JUST WHAT THE DOCTOR ORDERED Caroline Anderson
LABOUR OF LOVE Janet Ferguson
THE FAITHFUL TYPE Elizabeth Harrison
A CERTAIN HUNGER Stella Whitelaw

Discover the thrill of 4 exciting Medical Romances – FREE

FREE BOOKS FOR YOU

In the exciting world of modern medicine, the emotions of true love acquire an added poignancy. Now you can experience these gripping stories of passion and pain, heartbreak and happiness – with Mills & Boon absolutely FREE! AND look forward to a regular supply of Medical Romances delivered direct to your door.

❧ ❧ ❧

Turn the page for details of how to claim 4 FREE books AND 2 FREE gifts!

An irresistible offer from Mills & Boon

Here's a very special offer from Mills & Boon for you to becom a regular reader of Medical Romances. And we'd like to welcome you with 4 books, a cuddly teddy bear and a special mystery gift - absolutely FREE and without obligation!

Then, every month look forward to receiving 4 brand new Medical Romances delivered direct to your door for only £1.70 each. Postage and packing is FREE! Plus a FREE Newsletter featuring authors, competitions, special offers and lots more...

This invitation comes with no strings attached. Yo may cancel or suspend your subscription at any tir and still keep your FREE books and gifts.

It's so easy. Send no money now but simply comple the coupon below and return it today to:

Mills & Boon Reader Service, FREEPOST, PO Box 236, Croydon, Surrey CR9 9EL.

- - - - - - - - - NO STAMP NEEDED - - - - ✂

YES! Please rush me 4 FREE Medical Romances and 2 FREE gi Please also reserve me a Reader Service subscription. If I decide subscribe, I can look forward to receiving 4 brand new Medical Romances every month for only £6.80 - postage and packing FRE If I choose not to subscribe, I shall write to you within 10 days an still keep the FREE books and gifts. I may cancel or suspend my subscription at any time simply be writing to you. I am over 18 years of age. Please write in BLOCK CAPIT

Ms/Mrs/Miss/Mr _____ EF

Address _____

_____

_____ Postcode _____

Signature _____

mps MAILING PREFERENCE SERVICE